The Bitter End

The Bitter End

A Love Story

ELISE LAPHAM

gatekeeper press™
Tampa, Florida

The Bitter End: A Love Story

Published by Gatekeeper Press
7853 Gunn Hwy, Suite 209
Tampa, FL 33626
www.GatekeeperPress.com

Library of Congress Control Number: 2023941356

ISBN (hardcover): 9781662941108
eISBN: 9781662941115

For My Parents
Their never-ending love story continues to inspire us.

To My Children
Ian and Amanda
Thank you for being two of my biggest cheerleaders.

Gratitude
For My Friends and Family

I'm grateful for my "Soul Sisters" (you know who you are) and for the "Boys of Summer." Thanks for your friendship and a lifetime of summer memories.

Thanks to my editor, Bettye Underwood, at Red Pen Edits, for her guidance, advice, kindness, and patience.

And a special thank you to Francesco Saverio Tarantini (www.fraxav.com) for capturing the spirit of the beach house with your beautiful cover design.

This is a love story—some of it based on real events—part pure fiction.

Contents

The Bitter End

FILLED WITH ANGER and regret after her alcoholic husband comes home in a rage and admits to having an affair, Lilly Conroy decides to take her son John to spend the summer at her family's beach house in Mattapoisett, Massachusetts, near Cape Cod. Here she hopes to find the courage to reinvent herself and focus on creating a new life away from a marriage that was filled with anger, regret, and disappointment.

As the summer unfolds, the heat is on.

Old flames are reignited, but what is found could be lost again. As sparks fly and passion burns, a secret looms that could ultimately tear two people apart . . .

Chapter 1

Summer Begins

June 1990

I T WAS TIME.

She had been holding on to the pain for too long.

Lilly knew it.

Kate knew it.

John knew it.

It was time to let go, shut the door on the past, and move on.

Now if she could only do it.

Lilly Conroy turned to her eleven-year-old son, John, who sat beside her in the car.

"Are you ready to roll?" she asked.

"Yes!" John turned to her with a big smile on his face. She could feel the excitement in his voice.

"Ok, then—let's get going!"

Lilly started the engine of her new black Volvo station wagon, backed out of the driveway of their home in Mount Kisco, New York, and headed east. While summer was her favorite time of year, this year it meant more than warmer weather. For her, this first day of summer marked the start of a new chapter—a new season in her life. After two years of messy arguments, custody battles, and alimony disputes, her divorce from Roger Wentworth had been finalized, and she was ready to leave her marriage in the past and begin life again as Lilly Conroy.

John, as always, was happy to be out of school and looking forward to spending the summer at the beach house. As they drove along the highway, he talked non-stop about all the things he wanted to do this summer.

"Mom, I really want to learn how to sail this summer and go fishing. Do you think we could ride our bikes to Gulf Hill for ice cream tonight?

"I'm sure we'll have time to check out the old sailboat down at the beach today and maybe we'll have time for a bike ride and ice cream, if we get unpacked before dinner. But don't worry, John, you'll have all summer to sail, fish, and ride your bike. We don't have to do everything the first day!"

She was happy that he hadn't complained about not going back to the summerhouse in Newport, Rhode Island, where they had summered all his life.

Lilly looked in the rearview mirror as she came to a stop sign and gently swept her hair from her eyes. She'd cut her long, honey-blond hair into a chic bob two weeks ago and was still getting used to her new look. Sometimes it was startling to see the reflection she saw staring back at her.

Her hairdresser had kept Lilly's bangs long and swept to the side of her face. They accented her soft brown eyes and gave her a sultry look. She felt like a new person—the new haircut was refreshing—and practical. Short hair would be easy to maintain at the beach this summer.

At thirty-eight, she'd started to become concerned about "looking old," and felt a short cut and highlights might help her look and feel younger. She thought about the classic, black, one-piece, halter-top bathing suit she'd bought at Bloomingdales. She dreaded shopping for bathing suits, but the salesperson had assured her the suit highlighted her figure. It had become harder to maintain her weight as she neared forty, which is why she did her best to watch her diet and went to the gym every morning to keep off the pounds.

As she steered on to the highway ramp, she glanced at the clock on the dashboard. It was just past 10:00 a.m., and Lilly hoped traffic wouldn't be too bad when they reached Boston in the early afternoon and headed to the south shore.

John looked up from his backpack after double-checking to make sure he had brought along his summer reading books.

"Mom, how long will it take us to get there? I want to go to the beach."

"We should be there by two, but you'll need to help me unload the car. We have a lot to unpack before we can go swimming."

John was starting to get restless after two hours in the car.

"OK, but can we make it quick? I want to sign up for sailing lessons. Maybe I'll win a trophy in the regatta, just like you and Uncle Mark did."

Lilly didn't have the heart to point out to him that he'd need a lot more experience before he could win the regatta.

"Why don't you get a jump on your summer reading while I'm driving? Remember, you need to spend an hour a day keeping up with your schoolwork this summer."

John was just entering middle school and earned good grades, but preferred sports over academics. A born leader, he was naturally athletic and always organizing some type of game for the neighborhood kids—street hockey and baseball were his favorites. Getting him to sit still and focus on homework was always a challenge.

He was the spitting image of his father, with wavy dark hair and brown eyes that reflected the light in such a way that they almost looked green at times. Lilly's friends always commented on how handsome he was.

But while John took after Roger in looks, Lilly was working hard to make sure he didn't follow in his father's footsteps in other ways.

His older sister, Kate, was the better student. She looked like Lilly, sharing the same petite physique and honey-blond hair. Her eyes were as blue as the sky. She had a warm smile and a gentle laugh, although she tended to be more of an introvert.

Kate wouldn't be joining them until later in the week; she had just finished her sophomore year at NYU and had been studying abroad in Greece for a semester. Lilly missed her desperately and was counting the days until her return.

She and Kate had a special bond. While Lilly didn't want to rush the summer along, she was looking forward to Kate joining them at the beach house in Mattapoisett. Her flight would land at Logan Airport on the Fourth of July, which was also Lilly's birthday.

Kate had taken the divorce hard and worried about her mother. Lilly knew traveling to Europe would be good for Kate and she could sense a big change in Kate's personality during her most recent call.

She sounded upbeat and positive for the first time in many months as she filled Lilly and John in on her travels, the food, the beautiful scenery, and the people she had met in Athens.

Lilly suspected there might also be a new boyfriend in the picture. Kate often talked about a student named Brandon and during the last call Kate had asked if he could come to Mattapoisett for a visit this summer. She was looking forward to meeting Brandon—but more importantly, she couldn't wait to see Kate in person and hug her close.

While Kate and Lilly were very close, the same could not be said of Kate's relationship with her father. Their relationship had become strained in recent years when Roger's drinking and womanizing began to take a heavy toll on his relationships at home.

Roger was a highly successful attorney, and provided a very comfortable life for his family, but during the past five years his work became all-consuming. He had become a workaholic—and an alcoholic. Lilly resented him for it. Roger also tried to make Lilly feel guilty, blaming her when both kids chose to live with her after the divorce. He accused her of ruining his relationship with them and threatened to stop making tuition payments if the kids didn't spend part of the summer with him this year. Reluctantly, she agreed.

Lilly's pulse began to race, and her palms grew sweaty as she thought about Roger and how much he had changed. She felt her grip tighten on the steering wheel. The old stress response, anxiety and anger, began to build as she thought about how her marriage had unraveled during the past five years.

Roger had always been a handsome man, tall with jet-black hair and dark brown eyes, but in the past few years the alcohol had changed his behavior. He was often irritable, lashing out at her if he was under stress or overwhelmed with work. Lilly believed stress and unhealthy competition with his brothers, who were both lawyers at the family's law firm, created most of his stress and led to his drinking. He would always unwind with a cocktail or two when he got home, but over the years it grew to several drinks a night. She pleaded with him many times to stop drinking and spend more time with her and the children, but he seemed to have little to no interest.

The final straw had come when she found out Roger was having an affair with his twenty-eight-year-old paralegal. He had often been working at the office late at night. She had begun to suspect the late nights were, in fact, date nights. Her suspicions were confirmed when a friend of hers saw Roger at Legal Seafoods having dinner and drinks with a young woman on a night he claimed to be working.

It wasn't long before word of Roger's affair had spread from Manhattan to Mount Kisco. Lilly felt like the whole town knew what was going on. She felt humiliated—and embarrassed. It was clear to her that Roger had lost sight of what was most important—his family. His career had become his priority in life, which made Lilly both sad and resentful. She longed to be with someone else—someone who would value her, enjoy spending time with her and the kids . . . someone who looked forward to talking to her at the end of the day. She longed to be held.

Roger mostly ignored her or paid attention only when they were attending a client dinner or other work event. She felt like a trophy wife. That was about to change now that the divorce was final.

While she had enjoyed being home when the kids were little, she had finally finished her college degree and planned to look for an illustrator position in the fall. She felt like she was finally slowly coming back to life and creating a path for her future. She was hopeful this summer in Mattapoisett would bring her to a better place and was looking forward to rekindling her friendships with long-lost friends who she hadn't seen in almost twenty years. In many ways, she had started to feel young again . . . and it felt good.

As Lilly headed off Route 24 and began the drive along Route 95 toward Mattapoisett, she shut off the AC and opened the windows to smell the salt air. As a little girl growing up in New England, summer held special memories for Lilly. Her parents had inherited the beach house from her grandparents. Lilly and her older brother Mark grew up spending every summer in Mattapoisett. They learned to sail together and won the Angelica Yacht Club summer sailing championship three times as teenagers.

Mark lived on the West Coast with his family now, and her parents had retired to Florida. While the house was usually rented for the summer season, when Lilly asked if she could spend this summer in Mattapoisett, they had agreed without hesitation. She regretted not returning sooner and creating summer memories with her own kids in Mattapoisett, but Roger preferred the family's summer estate in Newport, Rhode Island.

Roger had become a law partner at a young age—a rising star at the Wentworth family's law firm. He was driven to succeed and very competitive with his two older brothers, Nick and Kevin, who had joined the firm before him. The practice had doubled in size over the past ten years and now had offices in Washington, DC, and Charlotte, North Carolina, in addition to Boston, Rhode Island, and New York. Roger socialized with many wealthy clients as a member of the Newport Golf Club, and several CEOs, CFOs, and private equity firm partners owned summer homes near theirs and had become neighbors, if not friends.

Lilly preferred Mattapoisett. Life was simpler there. Unlike the mega mansions, egos, glitz, and glamour of Newport, Mattapoisett was a quaint seaside village that sat along Buzzards Bay, across from Cape Cod and sixty miles south of Boston.

But there were other reasons she had chosen to stay away from this special place. . . .

Chapter 2

A Trip Down Memory Lane

L ILLY BEGAN TO think back to that one special summer over twenty years ago as she turned down Sea Street onto Shore Drive and familiar sights came into view.

As they drove past Ned Point Lighthouse, she slowed down and pointed out the Coast Guard Station to John. She could hear the seagulls and started to breathe in the smell of the Mattapoisett ocean air. She welcomed the wind on her face as the breeze blew through the windows and they turned the final corner onto Harbor Point Road.

Most of Mattapoisett's population consisted of longtime summer residents. Old cottages with cedar shingles, the summer homes of generations of families, dotted the unspoiled coast. There were no public beaches, and only one hotel in the center of town with the unimaginative name of The Mattapoisett Inn & Tavern. While Mattapoisett wasn't a well-known destination for tourists like other areas of Cape Cod, it was considered one of the best-kept secrets for Boston-area families and mariners who grew up sailing and fishing there.

Lilly hadn't been back to the beach house in a long time, but she cherished the home that had been in her family for three generations. It was the last connection she had to her childhood, which is why she had always dreamed of returning one day. She wished her children were younger and could have enjoyed summers in the Point Connett neighborhood. Sometimes referred to as "The Point" by the locals, it was a little spit of beach that jutted out of Mattapoisett on the south side of town: home to Ned Point Lighthouse, about forty cottages, and the Bitter End Yacht Club, a small family-friendly sailing club at the rocky shoreline with breathtaking views of Buzzards Bay.

As she rounded the bend, the old cottage came into view. The house sat on a little sandy hill overlooking Buzzards Bay. She smiled as she took in the view and realized the house looked much the same as she remembered it. It was a large cottage dating back to 1932, with gray clapboard shingles, black shutters, a large wraparound porch, and four old white Adirondack chairs facing the bay. She pulled into the circular seashell driveway in front of the house, took a deep breath, and exhaled. She was home again.

She parked the car, stepped onto the driveway, and made her way to the weathered front porch. The seashells crunched beneath her feet as John followed behind her. She unlocked the door, stepped inside the living room and immediately felt the warmth and familiarity of her childhood home. The house held a lifetime of memories. She scanned the room. Lilly's mother had recently updated the furnishings with an oversized white slip-covered couch and matching chairs from Pottery Barn, but much of the house still looked the same. There were family photographs on the mantle above the fireplace, playing cards and games for rainy days on the side table, and a bookcase filled with romance and mystery novels. It was as if time had stood still. She pictured her parents playing cards with their friends and enjoying cocktails. Her dad's favorite was Jack Daniels on the rocks with the "peel of a lemon."

She suddenly felt a sense of peace wash over her that she hadn't felt in a very long time. John quickly ran past her, racing upstairs to check out his bedroom. Thoughts of July 4, 1969, started to fill Lilly's mind . . . although they had never really left. Her mind began to wander back in time—and to him.

She'd never forgotten him.

He had been her soulmate.

Her one and only.

Time had not healed the old wounds she carried with her.

Her heart ached with a bittersweet longing as she opened the windows and felt the warm summer breeze fill the room.

In her mind's eye, she could still see his face, the way his eyes sparkled when he spoke of his dreams to become a doctor when he returned home from Vietnam . . . the warmth of his touch when he held her close the day he left.

Even after all these years, she felt an inexplicable bond with Paul Fletcher, an invisible thread that connected their souls.

She closed her eyes and memories from the Summer of '69

came flooding back as if it was yesterday. The soft whispers of nostalgia started to bring her back to those moments in time.

The fun, the laughter, the innocence, and the love.

A tear escaped and trickled down her cheek as she sat on the window seat in the front hallway and looked out to the ocean, white sailboats dotting the horizon.

Chapter 3

The Day Begins

The Beach House
July 4, 1969

LILLY AWOKE TO the sound of The Rolling Stones blaring from her older brother Mark's car radio outside. She turned to face the warm summer breeze blowing through her bedroom window and saw the sun glistening on the ocean waters.

"Mark, turn that radio down!"

The screen door slammed shut as her father walked out onto the porch with a cup of coffee. Her bedroom was on the second floor, so she had a bird's-eye view of everything going on down below. Mark was revving the engine of his 1960 silver Mustang convertible. He was parked in the circular seashell driveway and had gotten out of the car to rub a spot off the hood.

She could hear her father's voice begin to rise. "It's not even 7:00 a.m. You're going to wake up the whole neighborhood. Your sister is still sound asleep!"

"Sorry, Dad! It's a beautiful day and I don't know why everyone is wasting it in bed. I'm heading over to pick up Charlotte. Tell Mom I'll be back for breakfast and tell my lazy little sister to rise and shine! It's her birthday, and besides, we've got to get ready for the regatta."

Lilly sat up and watched from her bed as her father turned and walked into the house, shaking his head. She and her brother were close to their parents, but Mark's high school and college years had been a challenge for them. He was always on the move, off to meet friends, and often bringing his ever-expanding entourage back to the house. Their mother hoped there would be some much-needed peace and quiet now that Mark was spending more time with his girlfriend, Charlotte.

Lilly heard a soft knock on her bedroom door.

"Honey, it's time to get up. Breakfast is ready, and you and Mark need to get down to the pier for the regatta." Her mother had a wonderfully sweet voice and was always cheerful.

Lilly didn't turn to face the door. She simply laid in bed, looking out the window. She blinked back the tears that had started to form in the corner of her eyes. She didn't want her mother to see that she'd been crying . . . again.

"I'll be down in a few minutes, Mom," Lilly called out before burying her head deep inside the pillow and drawing the sheets up around her head.

Today was the Fourth of July and her eighteenth birthday, but she was in no mood to celebrate.

She had been crying every night for a week. Each passing

day brought her boyfriend Paul's departure closer. He had just returned from boot camp at Camp Pendleton, and they had only a few short days together until he traveled to Fort Bragg for combat training before heading to Vietnam. His lifelong dream was to go to medical school to become a doctor and he had signed up to serve as a medic. She threw back the sheets, slowly sat up, and started thinking about the day ahead as she headed to the bathroom adjacent to her room to wash up and put on her bathing suit.

She washed her face, brushed her teeth, and swept her long honey-blond hair into a ponytail. Her face was tan and had a summer glow.

The day would be busy; after the regatta ended in the afternoon there'd be just enough time to shower and change for the July Fourth clambake down at the yacht club, followed by a bonfire on the beach after sunset and finally, fireworks.

She'd participated in this summer tradition since she was a little girl. Being born on the Fourth of July made her birthdays extra special. Every year, the parents all looked forward to dinner and dancing at the yacht club, while the younger kids and teenagers headed to the beach for the bonfire. She felt excited, but increasingly anxious about the day ahead, as she looked in the mirror. She stepped back, turned, checked her trim figure in the mirror, and headed downstairs.

Tonight, would be special. She and Paul were going to the bonfire and spending the evening together. She wanted to spend as much time with him as possible before he headed to Vietnam.

She felt more afraid about his tour of duty with each passing day, worrying that she might not ever see him again once he left.

She'd been madly in love with him for two years. It began as a summer romance but had grown into so much more during the past year.

While they initially kept in touch during the school year with letters and phone calls, this year Paul had bought a used car, a blue Chevy Camaro that he was always tinkering with. Lilly loved riding in it with the top down during the warmer months.

Having his own car made it easier for him to visit Lilly on the weekends in Brookline, just outside of Boston, where she lived with her family in the offseason. She had a confirmed Saturday night date with him every week—movies, shows, concerts, football games—it had been a whirlwind, but she had never been happier.

Wearing white shorts and a crisp white T-shirt over her swimsuit, Lilly clambered down the worn knotty pine stairs and joined her parents and Mark and his girlfriend, Charlotte, at the breakfast table, where her mom had placed heaping platters of scrambled eggs, bacon, toast, and a big pot of coffee.

"Happy birthday, Lilly!" her father shouted when she entered the room. "Let's sing before the day begins and we all scatter."

With that, they all broke into a cheerful and very loud rendition of *Happy Birthday*. Her mother smiled lovingly at her, and her dad brimmed with pride as he looked at his now eighteen-year-old daughter who would be attending Skidmore in the fall.

He reached in his pocket and pulled out a beautifully wrapped box with a yellow ribbon on it. "It's your eighteenth birthday, and your mother and I wanted to get you something special." He handed her the box and smiled broadly.

Lilly turned to her mother, who nodded happily. As she pulled the yellow ribbon away and opened the silver wrapping paper, she saw a familiar name on the box inside—DeScenza's.

DeScenza's was a well-known jeweler in the Boston area, where her father always shopped for gifts on special occasions.

She opened the box and saw a beautiful silver necklace with a ruby—her birthstone. She held it up and admired it, then looked over at her parents.

"It's beautiful! I'll cherish it and will always wear it on my birthday. Thank you both!" She got up and gave them each a kiss before gently placing the necklace back in the box.

As Lilly looked around the table at her loving family, a smile broke out on her face, and she felt happy.

Little did she know it was the beginning of a day she would never forget. Even now, all these years later, she remembered every detail. That fateful day from long ago had begun to unfold.

Chapter 4

The Regatta

"COME ON, LILLY, let's get going. The regatta will begin soon, and we need to get out to the mooring and get the sails up."

After finishing breakfast in record time, Mark got up from the table, grabbed his grey Boston College sweatshirt from the back of his chair, and headed out the door with Charlotte. Lilly took one last sip of her coffee and quickly stood.

"I'll put your necklace in your room for you, dear."

"Thanks, Mom." Lilly hugged her mother again.

Lilly turned and called out as she headed toward the door.

"Thanks for breakfast and the birthday gift. We'll see you later this afternoon!"

Her father followed behind her.

"Good luck, kids!" he yelled and waved from the porch. "We'll be watching from the pier." Lilly's father always enjoyed the July Fourth Regatta. As a teenager, he had sailed in the races with a friend and had more than a few sailing trophies on the mantle from those long-ago days when he was their age.

Lilly practically had to run to keep up with her brother. Charlotte would be watching the Regatta with their parents and other spectators from the pier.

"Wait up, Mark!" she called as she rushed to catch up with him. "What's your hurry?"

"I want to get out to the mooring and check a few things on the boat before the race starts. I'm a little worried about the rip in the mainsail that Dad fixed."

The boat had been in their family for decades. Like most families on Point Connett, they owned a classic twenty-foot Original Beetle Cat, a wooden sailboat first designed in 1921 and considered one of the first competitive racing boats in New England.

*   *   *

The sun shone brightly over the bay as they made their way down the sandy dirt road and arrived at Sandy Beach, where they would grab their rowboat and head out to the mooring. As they crossed over the dunes, Lilly saw Paul launching his boat from the pier. He looked so handsome, tan and muscular from working all summer at the boatyard. He had blond hair, which had turned bleached blond from the sun and wore a pair of Ray-Ban aviator sunglasses. His bare back was turned to her as he raised the sails on his boat, which gave her time to stand quietly and admire his physique.

She walked closer and stood directly above him on the pier. Lilly cleared her throat to get his attention.

"Good morning, sailor. It's a beautiful day for a regatta!"

He quickly turned and saw her standing above.

"Good morning, birthday girl!" He stood up in the boat, secured his lines, and jumped onto the pier. "I want to be the first person to give you a birthday kiss!"

"You're too late—another man has already kissed me this morning."

Reaching her, he playfully put his arms around her waist. "I'm jealous. Who was the lucky guy who got to give my beautiful girl a kiss on her eighteenth birthday?"

One hand rose to pull off his sunglasses. She melted as he looked at her intently with his deep blue eyes before drawing her close to him in a warm hug.

She laughed. "An older man, and someone I love very much. Luckily for you, it was my father!"

"In that case, it's OK." Paul leaned in and kissed her briefly, then brushed his lips against her cheek and whispered in her ear.

"I love you, Lilly Conroy. Happy eighteenth birthday. I have a special present for you. I'll give it to you tonight at the bonfire, OK?"

Her heart began to race, and she felt butterflies in her stomach whenever he kissed her. While they had been dating for two years, they had never made love, and it was getting harder and harder to resist taking that next step.

She needed him and wanted him more and more each day.

Those random thoughts of longing were quickly quelled by the shrill sound of the horn from the end of the pier, signaling that the race was about to begin.

"Are you two lovebirds interested in actually racing today, or do I need to find another crew member?" Mark had walked down the pier and sounded annoyed.

"Sorry, Mark. Your sister distracted me from my duties. She has a way of doing that."

Paul gave Lilly's hand a goodbye squeeze and ran off to his boat, where his friend Roger Wentworth waited for him.

Roger and Paul had been friends since childhood and still spent a lot of time together, although that had started to change when Lilly and Paul's relationship grew more serious. She never really liked Roger and questioned how the two of them could be such good friends. Roger was good-looking, smart, and a star athlete at Harvard, where he played football. He was also quite full of himself, and his ego had only gotten bigger now that he had been admitted to Harvard Law School. He was following his father's footsteps and would surely join the family law firm in Boston once he graduated. Lilly felt he was conceited, too proud of himself, and vain.

Paul always defended Roger and insisted to Lilly that beneath that brash exterior, Roger was a very nice guy. She wasn't so sure, but she did agree that Roger could be fun to be around when he wasn't bragging—he was the life of the party and brought excitement with him wherever he went. But she still didn't trust him.

Lilly was wary of Roger. She'd never told Paul about the

night last summer when Roger got drunk at a party and made a pass at her. Roger insisted on walking her home that night, since Paul was visiting his grandparents in Boston that weekend and wasn't around. She'd innocently thought he was simply trying to be a good friend and look out for her, but when they got to her doorstep, he leaned in and forcibly kissed her. She immediately pushed him away before slipping inside.

Not surprisingly, Roger apologized the next day, blaming his inappropriate behavior on the alcohol. She accepted his apology and agreed it would be best not to tell Paul about what had happened.

In spite of Roger's sincere apology, she never looked at him the same way after that. She felt increasingly uncomfortable around him, especially when he was drinking. She kept her distance from him whenever possible.

Lilly shook her head, as if to chase away the thoughts that had started to intrude on what was otherwise shaping up to be a very special birthday. She watched Paul board his boat, gave Roger a half-hearted wave, then ran and caught up with her brother on the beach. They waded into the water, jumped into the rowboat, and headed to the mooring to set sail.

It was a hot summer day and the wind had picked up nicely. The fleet of twenty-four Beetle Cats were waiting behind the course line to begin the race that would take them across Buzzards Bay, with windward markings showing the participants where to turn to head to Falmouth and back across the Bay to the finish line at the Point Connett pier.

The sailors jockeyed for position before the horn blast signaled the start of the race, and then the Cats were off!

Paul and Roger, on the port side of Lilly and Mark's boat, started taunting them.

"We'll be ahead of you all the way!" yelled Paul as he made a turn around the first marking.

"We'll see about that!" Mark shouted back. He let the sails out to catch the wind while Lilly pulled up the center board and adjusted the rudder. They were picking up speed and passed Paul and Roger as they made the second turn.

Three other boats behind them were gaining on them, so they tacked again and headed back toward Mattapoisett. Roger and Paul were closing in.

The two boats stayed in the lead all the way to the finish line, where Lilly could see the swarm of summer residents watching from the pier.

Suddenly, one of the Beetle Cats crashed into the starboard side of Mark and Lilly's boat, sending them off course. The boat began to keel, and before Lilly knew it, she was in the water.

Mark yelled at the skipper and crew responsible for the crash while Lilly was treading water and trying to get back to the boat, but the wind had picked up and the current was pushing against her in what almost felt like a riptide. She heard a splash behind her and turned to see Paul swimming toward her.

"Hold on, Lilly. I'll grab the line and get you back to the boat."

Roger added to the chaotic scene, first yelling at Mark to give way so he could pass and then yelling at Paul to get back on board.

"Fletcher, what the hell are you doing?" he angrily shouted. "We can still win. Get back on board before it's too late! She'll be fine!"

Mark headed away from the finish line toward his sister. He was concerned there was a riptide forming.

"You didn't have to jump in, Paul," Lilly chided him. "I know how to swim."

He held out a line for her to grab. "Did you think I would sail on by while the woman I love just got thrown overboard in the middle of Buzzards Bay? Don't you know there are sharks in these waters?"

Lilly laughed at the thought of shark-infested waters in Mattapoisett. The only large mammals found in Buzzards Bay were seals. She looked at Paul and smiled. He was so sweet, loving, and caring. She felt like the luckiest girl alive to be spending this day with him.

They joined hands in the water, side by side, with their bodies stretched out as they floated. Paul squeezed her hand and looked over at her while they waited for Mark to bring the boat alongside them.

Lilly began to tread water and slowly moved in close to playfully plant a kiss on his wet, salty cheek. "You're a real gentleman, Paul. I think I'll keep you by my side."

Roger stood up in the boat with his arms folded across his chest, clearly unhappy at the scene unfolding in the water. "I hope you two lovebirds know you just cost me this year's trophy!"

Lilly and Paul burst out laughing.

"We can win next year, Roger!" Paul called out, laughing. "When the war is over, I'll make it up to you!"

Roger shook his head and began to sail toward them.

Mark held out his hand to bring Lilly back on board, while Paul swam back to the boat where Roger had begun to adjust the sails so they could head back to shore.

A final blast of the horn from the pier indicated the race was over. The two boats headed in together, sailing side by side.

Chapter 5

Racing Against Time

AFTER THE REGATTA, Lilly went back to the cottage and enjoyed lunch on the front porch with her parents. They sat in the Adirondack chairs and laughed at the morning's events. While her father had always been a competitive sailor, as time went by, he focused more on enjoying life with his family at the beach house rather than challenging his son and daughter to always come in first.

After lunch, Lilly and Paul rode their bikes over to the Gulf Hill ice cream stand, where they shared a banana split—one of their favorite weekly traditions.

When she returned home, Lilly went upstairs for a quick nap and then relaxed in a cool bubble bath, thinking about the night ahead. Butterflies fluttered in her stomach as she daydreamed about Paul and all that was to come.

Tonight would be special, and she wanted to look perfect. After all, this was one of the last nights they would have together before Paul left for training camp. She'd bought a new summer dress: a short chiffon in periwinkle blue printed with little white seashells that complemented both her tan and her waistline.

She turned on the radio and listened to the Top 40 while she curled her hair. "Sugar, Sugar" by The Archies was playing and put her in a playful mood.

Her mood had been elevated since the race. She smiled as she applied a little mascara and lip gloss. As she looked in the mirror to check her reflection, she heard the front door open and voices downstairs. Paul had arrived . . . it was time. Her palms felt clammy, and she noticed her hands were shaking as she reached for her purse. The anticipation and anxiety she felt were starting to show.

Her mother called to her from downstairs. "Lilly, Paul is here!"

"I'll be right there!" She grabbed her small white purse and opened the bedroom door. She stopped at the top of the stairway and saw Paul standing in the foyer opposite her mother and father.

He held a small bouquet of wildflowers in his hand and looked as handsome as ever. He was almost six feet tall and towered over her petite mother as he stood at the bottom of the stairs. He wore a light blue collared shirt that complimented his slate-blue eyes. The short sleeves showed off his muscular tan arms. He wore crisp white slacks and tan loafers. She couldn't take her eyes off him. He stared up at her for what seemed like a very long time. Their eyes locked, and he seemed to struggle to find his voice. He cleared his throat and finally began to speak.

"You look beautiful."

She smiled at him and started down the stairs. Her parents beamed as he handed her the bouquet.

"Happy birthday, Lilly."

She gently took the bouquet from his hands and looked down as she smelled the beautiful summer flowers, daisies, and pink beach plum roses.

"Thank you, Paul."

The sound of her mother's voice interrupted the magical moment. "Lilly, I'll put these in a vase for you and set them on your nightstand so you can admire them after you get home. You two had better get going if you want to get to the clambake before all the lobster is gone!"

Lilly's father leaned in to give her a kiss. "Have a great time!"

"Thanks, Dad. Goodnight!"

Paul and Lilly went out the front door and strolled down the sandy beach road lined with pink summer rosebushes on their way to the yacht club, holding hands and laughing as they recalled the comical ending to the regatta.

They continued to hold hands after arriving at the clambake, intertwined and holding on tight to each other, only letting go to eat. She was filled with anticipation as the clock perched on the wall ticked away the last precious moments they had left together. It was a constant reminder that time was slipping away.

She wondered if Paul heard it and if he felt the same way. She wanted to cherish every last moment they had together. They socialized with Mark and Charlotte and a few other friends on the patio: longtime sweethearts, Sarah and Lewis; Charlie and his girlfriend, Joanne; and others, as they enjoyed their dinner. A local band provided music on the wide rolling lawn that led out to the ocean, and a few couples were dancing on the square bluestone patio that served as a dance floor.

Paul stood up from the table after they finished dessert and once again reached for Lilly's hand. "May I have this dance?"

She rose, and together they walked to the dance floor. In a change of pace, the band was playing The Righteous Brothers' "Unchained Melody."

He held her close and his embrace tightened as they danced. He softly whispered in her ear.

"Let's skip the bonfire and head down to the little private beach near Oyster Bay. I have a present for you and want to stop by my house to get it."

She smiled up at him, eager for the song to end so they could leave and spend the rest of the night alone together.

When the song was over, they snuck away and walked down to the water toward Paul's family's cottage that was situated on the farthermost cliff.

They walked around to the back of the house where Paul gestured for Lilly to sit down in one of the patio chairs. His parents were still at the yacht club and the house was dark.

"I'll be right back—just wait here." He went inside through the back door, reappearing a few minutes later carrying a flashlight, two blankets, and a bottle of wine with two plastic wine glasses inverted over the top.

"Now, let's go celebrate your eighteenth birthday, Lilly!" He clasped her hand, and they giddily ran down the road.

Just before the entrance to a private, narrow hidden path that led to a little spit of sand called Baby Beach, they both turned toward the yacht club. They heard strains from the band playing in the distance and saw the faint glow of the bonfire further down the beach. It was a starry summer night.

"I hope you don't mind missing the bonfire, but I wanted to be alone with you tonight, Lilly." Paul kicked off his shoes and spread the blanket on the sand in front of the private cove.

She looked up at the full moon and its reflection on the bay before settling onto the blanket with him and turning to look into his eyes. "Of course, I don't mind. There isn't any place else I'd rather be than alone with you right now, Paul."

As the waves gently lapped the shore, the moonlit beach was bathed in a soft ethereal glow. The cool breeze carried the scent of salt air.

His upper body leaned forward, and she met him halfway for a lingering kiss. It started gently, but quickly became urgent. Lilly felt disappointed when he broke away.

He reached into his pocket and handed her a small white box tied with a blue ribbon. She'd forgotten all about the gift he mentioned he had for her.

"I wanted to give you something special tonight," he said. "This is just a little token. When I get back from my tour of duty, we'll trade up for the real thing and make it official."

She untied the ribbon, opened the box, and saw a delicate

heart-shaped gold ring with a small diamond nestled in the center.

"Paul, it's beautiful! I love it!" She gently removed it from the box, placed it on the ring finger of her right hand, and extended her arm in front of her, admiring how it looked on her finger.

"No, that's not right."

Lilly looked at him, puzzled.

He reached for her right hand, gently removed the ring, then slipped it onto the ring finger of her left hand. "This is where it belongs. I want to marry you, Lilly. Consider this a pre-engagement ring. I hope we can pick up where we left off when I get back. I hope you'll wait for me and give me the chance to formally propose to you."

Even in the moonlight, she could see the love and resolve in his eyes.

"I love you, Lilly, and I want to spend my life with you. I hope you'll wait for me. When I get back, I'll propose to you properly with a beautiful diamond and I hope you'll say 'yes.'"

She looked down at the ring, her eyes filling with happy tears.

"Of course, I'll wait for you! And forget about trading up! This ring is too special for that. I won't even take it off until you're back and I have a wedding ring to wear alongside it. I love you, Paul, and I want to be your wife."

Paul reached for the bottle. "Time for some wine! Although, I wish it was champagne."

"It's a celebration, but wine will have to do." he said, as he uncorked the bottle and poured them each a glass.

Paul filled a glass halfway and handed it to her, then filled the other glass. Lilly held both glasses for him while he re-stopped the bottle with the corkscrew. He took one of the glasses from her and pressed it against hers. "Here's to a lifetime together."

She beamed. "A lifetime together," she repeated. She loved the way that sounded.

When they finished their wine, Paul set their glasses down, then clasped her hands tightly in his. He desperately wanted to make love to her and was afraid he might not ever get another chance. He didn't let it show, but he was aware of the casualty statistics, and that the odds of him coming home in a pine box were pretty good. He worried about dying—but he also knew that courage wasn't about having no fear, it was about moving ahead despite your fears.

He wasn't sure how he felt about the war, but he knew he loved his country and believed in democracy. He also knew that he didn't want to leave without making love to Lilly. He wanted her to be his and his alone, whether it be for fifty years, fifty days, or fifty minutes. He wanted to know what it would feel like to be closer to her than he'd ever been before . . . to know each plane of her body, her most sensitive areas . . . to be her first and only lover.

Lilly felt the same way.

Their desire for each other was reflected in the way they kissed, becoming more and more passionate as they tore at each other's clothes. He broke away from her lips to plant little gentle kisses all along her throat. "Oh, Lilly. You don't know how much I want you tonight," he whispered in her ear.

"I know, Paul. I want you too."

Paul cupped her face with his palm. "Lilly? Are you sure? It's important to me that you be sure."

She nodded. "I've never been so sure of anything in my life."

He genlty pulled her backward onto the blanket and began slowly kissing her. His lips were moist and warm as he kissed her cheeks, neck, shoulders and slowly undressed her. He wanted her as much as she wanted him.

After they made love, Lilly leaned over him.

"Paul, when you're away and feeling lonely, remember tonight and remember how we feel about each other. That feeling will never go away—no matter how far away you are, I will be here. Waiting for you."

Lilly lay in Paul's arms, the blanket wrapped around them, looking at the stars and listening to the waves crashing just a few yards away. They whispered promises of forever as they held each other tight, and she realized before tonight that she had been only half-alive.

She wanted to be with him forever. It felt so natural, so right.

He stroked her hair while gently kissing her cheek. "I love you, Lilly. I'll never forget this night."

She snuggled closer to him, and his arm tightened around her. "I just wish . . ." She choked back a sob, cursing herself for ruining the moment with her fears, but she couldn't help it. Tears ran down her cheeks at the thought of him leaving for Vietnam in the morning. She had started to have nightmares of him being hurt and calling out for her—but in her dreams no matter how fast she ran she couldn't reach him.

One by one, he kissed her tears away. "I need you to be brave, Lilly. Please don't worry."

"I promise to do everything I can to stay safe and come home to you. And if you'll have me, we'll get married. Remember, it's considered a hardship tour of duty and I only have to make it for twelve months. It'll go by fast. Time always does. You'll be busy with school. It's all going to be OK."

Hearing him talk about their future gave her confidence that he *would* return to her and hold her like this again. . . .

Suddenly they heard a loud bang as the sky lit up with the thunderous sound of fireworks from the pier. The annual display had begun. Lilly's breath caught in her throat. They sat together, wrapped in the blanket, and watched the fireworks as Paul shifted to her side.

As the night air cooled, they slowly got dressed and quietly talked about their plans for the future: the places they wanted to go, the things they wanted to do.

They snuggled under the blanket and looked up at the night sky that had grown smoky from the fireworks. They fell asleep wrapped in each other's arms as the chilly night air set in. Lilly woke up, shivering.

Paul rubbed her bare back to warm her up. "I'd better get you home. I don't want my future wife to catch cold!" With that they slowly got to their feet. Paul wrapped the blanket around Lilly's shoulders. They headed home hand in hand well past midnight.

*   *   *

When they reached the front porch of her house, he took her in his arms and kissed her, whispering her name as they stood locked in an embrace. Lilly felt lighter than air. She planted one last kiss on his lips and whispered goodnight to him before opening the front door and slipping inside.

She quietly headed up the stairs to her room, not wanting to wake her parents, and collapsed on her bed. Looking over at Paul's beautiful summer flowers that her mother had placed on her nightstand, she drifted off to sleep feeling happy, peaceful, and content.

Chapter 6

The Send Off

MONDAY CAME ALL too soon. She awoke suddenly and sat up in bed bathed in sweat at 6:00 a.m. This was it. She suddenly realized their time together was over—at least for now. The day she'd dreaded for so long had finally come. Today he was leaving.

The joy and lightheartedness she'd felt all weekend with him was gone. She felt anxious.

She brushed her teeth and tied her hair in a ponytail, but the intrusive thoughts wouldn't let go. She buttoned her dress and smoothed it over her hips in an effort to still her shaking hands.

She checked her reflection in the mirror. She may have looked normal on the outside, but on the inside, she felt her whole world was about to unravel. The realm of "what-ifs" started to emerge again.

What if he gets killed? What if I never get to see him again, hold him, kiss him, be his wife and have children with him?

She dried the tears that filled her eyes and patted her face, then took one last glance in the mirror, her jaw set with determination.

Stop being selfish! she chided herself. She needed to be strong today, for Paul as well as for his parents. She knew they were just as worried as she was. Paul was being brave, showing no fear at the thought of what was to come; she needed to be brave like him and think positively!

* * *

Paul's mother had invited her to join them for breakfast before he took the bus to Boston to meet his military flight at Logan Airport. The day bloomed hot and sunny. Lilly wore the new white sundress she'd bought on sale at a small boutique shop in Brookline. She had saved this dress for this occasion. She wanted to look pretty for his send-off.

The four of them ate in almost complete silence for several minutes, the only sound being that of the silverware hitting the plates. Paul's father was the first to speak.

"You have a nice day to head out to Fort Bragg, Paul. Be sure to rest up on the bus and the plane—you'll be getting up early from now on!" Paul's father was doing a masterful job of concealing the fear he must have felt, unlike his wife, who had a worried look on her face as she looked over at Paul.

"If only you'd gone right to medical school after college instead of taking time off."

Lilly knew how Paul's mother felt. Taking a year off was long enough for the draft board to catch up with him and learn that he wasn't a student.

But Paul wanted to take some time off and work at the local neighborhood health clinic before starting medical school. He knew the long hours he would need to commit to studying and wanted to spend more time with Lilly before she left for college.

Paul's father cleared his throat and began to speak.

"Well, I served in World War II and I know what it's like to defend our country. I'm very proud of Paul. We can't just watch while the free world is threatened. He can finish medical school when he's back—the time will pass quickly for all of us."

Paul's mother looked across the table and over at her husband.

"This war is different from World War II. Our freedom was at stake. I just don't understand how sending our boys off to the jungle halfway around the world is going to help fight communism. I don't think we should be getting ourselves involved in other people's battles. I just don't understand it."

It was obvious to Lilly that Paul's parents were conflicted, like so many other people. She agreed with Paul's mother and wished the war would end, but she also knew that Paul would never be a draft dodger.

Paul put his hand on his mother's arm and attempted to reassure her.

"Don't worry mom, I'll be home before you know it!"

His mother raised a hand to cover her mouth and cleared her throat, then attempted a smile. Stella Fletcher was a beautiful, slender woman with steel-blue eyes and brown hair that she wore pinned in a French roll. Always fashionably dressed, this morning she wore a brown sleeveless blouse with cream-colored linen pants.

She looked down at her plate and took a sip of orange juice.

Mrs. Fletcher was inwardly struggling not to break down from worries about her only child going to serve in such an unpopular war.

As they made small talk for the rest of the meal, Lilly managed to control herself and even participated in the conversation a bit, but it was extremely difficult for her to try and pretend today was just like any other day.

Paul's mother rose and began to clear away the dishes. It was as if keeping busy would keep her from breaking down in front of him. When she returned to the table, Paul suddenly stood and wrapped her in a big hug. His mother held him tightly, as if she didn't want to let go.

His father was driving them to the bus terminal in Hyannis, where she and Paul would say goodbye. His mother surprised Paul with her next comment.

"I'll say my goodbyes here." Lilly suspected Mrs. Fletcher would be crying the moment they were gone.

Paul wore a brave façade, determined to fulfill his obligations as a brave soldier and holding steadfast to the fact that he would return home—alive.

"Now, Stella," Paul's father said. "Stop worrying. Paul will be fine. He'll come back to us just like I came back to you after my service."

"Don't worry about me, Mom. I'll write you every week, and before you know it, we'll all be one year older, and I'll be standing right here beside you." He squeezed her gently and then backed away, holding both her hands in his. Her eyes became visibly moist as she took one last look at her son.

He was her only child, and Lilly could only imagine how hard it was for her to let him go.

Every news report Lilly saw about the conflict intensified the nervousness she felt about the war. She realized how dangerous it was becoming for the soldiers stationed in Vietnam and watched the body bags being carried onto Blackhawk helicopters each morning on the news with the latest count of U.S. soldiers wounded, killed, or missing in action. Lilly prayed that Paul wouldn't be one of them.

Paul looked over at Lilly, and then at his mother, and could see the worry on their faces.

He gave them a stern lecture.

"Now, Mom, I don't want you or Lilly watching the news updates. No one knows what's really going on over there. You need to keep busy, and Lilly will need to stay focused on her schoolwork while I'm gone. Promise me you both will stop watching those morning news updates."

They slowly shook their heads, but neither his mother nor Lilly said a word. They both knew it was going to be hard not knowing where he was or how he was doing.

"OK, we'd better get going!" Paul's father took a last sip of coffee, stood from the table, and kissed his wife's cheek. "I'll be back in a few hours, honey." The reassuring squeeze he gave his wife's shoulder tugged at Lilly's heartstrings.

Paul grabbed his duffel bag. Lilly watched him lovingly. She couldn't stop looking at him as he prepared to leave. She also felt the familiar melancholy starting to set in.

Paul wore a gray T-shirt, green army fatigues, and heavy black military boots. He made a lighthearted comment on how he'd have to break them in before he got to Vietnam as the three of them walked to the car. After giving his mother one last embrace, he and Lilly slid into the back seat of his father's new blue Buick, Paul's mother blew him a kiss and waved as they pulled out of the driveway. Lilly was certain she saw her trembling. Paul kept looking back at her through the rear window until they rounded the bend and headed to Route 6.

His father turned on the local sports channel to get the latest baseball scores; last night the Boston Red Sox had played the New York Yankees at Fenway Park. Other than the radio announcer's voice giving the scores from last night's games, they rode in silence.

It took about an hour to get to Hyannis, but for Lilly it went by all too fast. Paul's father parked the station wagon in front of the terminal. They all got out of the car. Lilly discreetly moved several yards away to give Paul and his father a few private moments together.

Her eyes were fixed on the Fort Bragg bus, where all the soldiers were beginning to board. She turned in time to see Paul hug his father, and then his father stepped back and saluted Paul.

"I'll wait for you in the car, Lilly," Mr. Fletcher called out as Paul turned and walked toward her. "You two take your time with your goodbyes." He got back into the car, lowered the window, and turned the radio back on.

Paul took Lilly's hand, and together they approached the bus.

She looked around as Paul checked in with the bus driver, watching the young recruits and their families and sweethearts saying goodbye . . . just like her and Paul.

Paul loaded his duffel into the bus's luggage compartment and returned to her side. He held her hands in his and the two of them talked quietly, both promising to write frequently.

"Remember, Lilly, it's only twelve months. Time will go by fast. I'll do everything in my power to stay safe and come back to you. Nothing will keep me from getting back to where I need to be—with you."

Lilly was determined not to cry; she didn't want him to leave with the memory of her sobbing. Despite her promise to herself, tears began to form, and she feared she was on the verge of a complete emotional breakdown.

"I know, Paul. I will be busy with school—you're right it's only twelve months. We'll just need to stay focused on when you return and all the plans we've made. I will be okay; you're the one I'm worried about."

"Please, Lilly, don't worry about me. I will be back—I promise you that."

Suddenly the sound of the bus driver's voice broke into their conversation.

Standing by the luggage compartment, the driver cupped his mouth and shouted to the passengers who hadn't yet boarded.

"The bus for Fort Bragg will be leaving in three minutes, soldiers!" he bellowed loudly.

The driver sounded friendly rather than angry, Lilly thought.

She let out a little cough as black smoke bellowed from the back of the bus. Some of the young men said one last hurried goodbye, kissing their mothers, and doing a combination handshake and quick embrace with their fathers. Most of them paused to turn on the bottom step and wave before boarding the bus.

Lilly swallowed over a lump in her throat. She and Paul both looked over at the bus driver, then at each other. The moment she had dreaded for so long had finally arrived.

She stepped into his embrace, and he held her tightly as she blinked back tears, reminding herself of her promise not to cry. A sense of foreboding and fear suddenly overtook her. She bit down hard on her lower lip and forced herself to smile before pulling back to look into his slate-blue eyes.

They kissed, and then he pressed his lips against her eyelids, as if sensing her struggle to keep from crying.

"I love you, Lilly. You know I'll be thinking of you every day. The countdown starts today. I'll be back in just twelve months!"

He looked down as she handed him a wallet-sized photo. It was her senior class picture, the most recent photo she had of herself.

"Keep this with you, Paul. I don't want you to forget what I look like!" She rose on tiptoe to kiss his cheek.

"I love you, Paul. I promise to write every week and to wait for you. Be safe and please come back to me. I need you."

He kissed her lips one last time, then her forehead. "Thank you for the picture. I'll kiss it every night." He slipped it into his breast pocket, grabbed her hand, and gave it a squeeze.

"Goodbye for now, my love."

As many of the other soldiers had done, he paused on the steps of the bus to look back at her. Lilly stifled an anguished cry when he mouthed the words "I love you," and mouthed the same back to him.

"See you in twelve months, Lilly Conroy!"

Paul stood on the bottom step and blew her one last kiss. He was the last one on the bus. The driver closed the door before pulling off. Lilly ran alongside the bus with a few other people, mostly girlfriends of the young soldiers who had just boarded, frantically waving goodbye until the bus gained speed, turned onto Route 6, and left them behind in the distance.

Lilly had one final glimpse of Paul's handsome young face as he stuck his head out the window and waved to her. That image of him formed a forever imprint in her memory. She didn't know it at the time, but it would haunt her for years.

Chapter 7

Missing

THE REST OF the summer went by quickly. Before she knew it, it was Labor Day weekend, and Lilly's family was closing up the summer house and returning to Brookline.

She was about to start her freshman year at Skidmore College in Saratoga Springs, New York. The busy days of school shopping helped to pass the time, but Lilly missed Paul terribly. The days were long and the nights even longer.

She didn't know how she would make it another ten months, but she'd somehow gotten through the first two. She decided the best she could do was write to him nightly, even if she mailed the letters only two or three times a week.

She felt a sense of relief each time the mailman arrived and delivered a letter addressed to her from Marine Group 12, 1st Marine Air Wing, Lam Son. She would run up to her room and re-read each sentence at least a half dozen times. It helped her to feel close to him. His last letter sounded upbeat and positive. She wondered why he never wrote of the battles or the fighting in Vietnam, but then remembered he had told her all the mail would be censored, so he would not be able to share any specifics about the war when he wrote to her.

* * *

The day before she left for school, his latest letter arrived. As usual, she quickly ran up to her room to read it in private.

Dearest Lilly,

I miss you so much and appreciate all your letters!

I know you worry that your letters are boring and meaningless, but rest assured, they are not!

Your letters remind me of home—and of you. Please keep sharing all that you are doing each day while we're apart.

For a few minutes, when I read your letters, I'm taken far away from here. I'm not carrying hand grenades or guns or fighting in the jungle.

For a few minutes, I'm back home with you enjoying an ice cream, going sailing, or walking along the beach. It helps me feel normal—and happy.

I am trying to stay focused on doing the best job I can do for the soldiers in my platoon.

It's not easy being a medic; I feel so much responsibility and wonder if I'm even qualified to help—but I try my best each day.

As I write this letter, you must be getting ready to head to Skidmore. I wish I could be there to see you off to college—and to kiss you, hold you, and . . . love you!

I hope your first week at school goes well. Please don't worry about me—study hard—keep busy and I will see you soon my love!

Until then, I will see you in my dreams each night and carry you in my thoughts every minute of the day until I'm back home with you again.

Love,
Paul

Her fingers traced the inked lines. She slowly began the ritual she had grown accustomed to—meticulously refolding the letter, kissing the envelope, carefully reinserting his letter, and gently placing it over her heart while she said a prayer.

She opened the nightstand drawer and gently added it to the growing collection, re-wrapping the blue ribbon she tied around the pile. She cherished each letter and every day she could add another. It meant he was still alive.

She arrived at Skidmore a few days later, on Labor Day, and became fast friends with her roommate, Erika Franklin. Erika was from Fairfield, Connecticut. She was a petite girl with auburn shoulder-length hair and beautiful green eyes. She was friendly and outgoing, a social butterfly who had been nominated Freshman Class Officer within three weeks of arriving on campus. Lilly and Erika formed an immediate bond. While Lilly was more of an introvert, they had a lot in common. They were both art majors and both were separated from boyfriends who were overseas.

The difference was that Erika's boyfriend, an international government major, was studying abroad in Italy, not serving in Vietnam. But while she didn't share the same worries, Erika missed her boyfriend just as much as Lilly missed Paul. The comfort they brought to each other during those first few weeks helped them form a special bond. They shared stories with each other and often walked to the post office together after class.

When she wasn't in class, studying, or writing to Paul, Lilly immersed herself in all the college activities associated with being a freshman. Skidmore had been her first choice of colleges, and she'd been excited to receive her acceptance letter. The campus was absolutely beautiful, nestled on over eight hundred acres, with walking trails and modern dormitories.

The first month on campus as a freshman flew by. October meant cooler nights and a change of season. The autumn weather brought fall foliage and a vibrant tapestry of colors emerged across the campus.

She had struggled to keep from feeling nervous with each passing day since Paul left for Vietnam. She was trying to keep her promise to him and refrained from watching the news, but Vietnam War protests were beginning to take shape across college campuses and Skidmore was no exception.

She felt conflicted and torn about supporting the protestors when her boyfriend was serving overseas, stationed in Vietnam, and believed he was protecting his country and fighting for democracy.

*   *   *

Lilly was sitting in the window seat of her dorm room, wearing a sweatshirt and faded jeans. She was sketching the fall landscape for her introductory art class, lost in her thoughts.

She struggled to stay focused on her assignment and began to daydream. She thought about Paul, imagined his voice, his touch, and the way he made her heart flutter whenever he was close. While she did her best to keep busy, being apart was becoming harder with each passing day and she longed for the day when they would be together again.

Suddenly, a loud knock on her bedroom door interrupted her thoughts. She recognized the voice of Susie Lind, the resident assistant. Lilly rose from the window seat and opened the door.

"Lilly, your mother is on the house phone."

Lilly was confused. It was strange for her mother to be calling in the middle of the week; long distance was cheaper on the weekends. She felt a pit in her stomach . . . something must be wrong. Had her father become ill? Had Mark had an accident? Or . . .

The adrenaline began to kick in. Lilly ran barefoot down the hall toward the phone booth.

"Mom?" She heard the anxiety in her own voice. "Is everything OK?"

"I'm afraid not." Her mother's sweet voice was unusually soft. She sounded serious.

"What is it, Mom? Did something happen to Dad? Nana? Mark?" She didn't want to ask what she feared the most. *Was it Paul?*

"I'm so sorry, Lilly. Mrs. Fletcher called earlier today. She was terribly upset. Two Marines came to their home last night. Paul has been reported . . . he's . . . he's MIA, Lilly. Missing in action."

Lilly's hand rose to clutch at her throat. "No," she whispered. "No!" she repeated, more forcefully this time.

"He can't be missing. He just wrote me a letter. He said he was safe and would write again soon. No! He can't be missing, Mom, he *can't!*" By now she was shouting, and she got up from the small wooden bench that served as a seat in the phone booth. As if standing and yelling would somehow make what her mother was saying go away. It couldn't be true.

"Lilly, dear, please try to calm down and listen to me."

Lilly slid back onto the seat, leaning her head against the wall. The tears began to flow uncontrollably.

"We don't know for sure, but you should understand what this might mean. Your father went over to visit with the Fletchers this morning, shortly after they called. Paul was on a mission in Lam Son to evacuate wounded soldiers. Apparently, they came under heavy fire from the Vietnamese. He was on one of the two medical helicopters that were shot down. He's listed as missing in action, but Mrs. Fletcher said the Marines believe he was either captured or . . . or killed. None of the marines who were in the helicopters came back from the mission. It's been three days, dear."

"Does Mrs. Fletcher believe Paul is dead?" Lilly managed to ask through her sobs.

"She didn't say that word. She just asked us to pray for him."

Lilly doubled over, sobbing into the phone.

"Lilly, Dad and I are going to drive down to see you tomorrow. We know this is a shock, and we're worried about you. We're going to leave early and should be there late in the morning. I'm so sorry, honey. We're all so sad about this and are at a loss for words. I'm so concerned about Paul's poor parents. He was—*is* their only child. It all seems so unfair, and while I don't want to see Communism spread, I'm beginning to feel like so many others do . . . that we'll never win this war." She paused, as if waiting for Lilly to respond, but there was only silence on the other end of the line.

Lilly was in shock. Her hands trembled as she cradled the phone, and her legs felt weak as she tried to stand up and steady herself in the booth.

"Lilly, are you still there?" her mother asked. "Talk to me, honey. Lilly?"

"I . . . I can't, Mom. I can't talk right now. I just want to go back to my room. I need to be alone."

"I understand. I want you to call us if you need anything. Reverse the charges. We'll see you tomorrow morning."

Lilly slowly hung up the phone, sat down, and buried her face against her folded arms.

Three days ago. She'd received a letter from him just three days ago. She still had it on her dresser. As always, he'd written that he missed her terribly and that he looked at her photo every night before he fell asleep. Lilly soundlessly recited the last few words in his letter. *I love you, Lilly.*

Her soft cries gave way to loud screams as she began to sob uncontrollably. The phone booth began to feel claustrophobic. She kicked open the door, and her cries floated into the hall. Doors along the corridor opened, her friends ran down the hall and surrounded her, some tentatively speaking her name. Lilly vaguely hearing the whispers:

"Her boyfriend is in Vietnam. She must have gotten some bad news."

"Oh, my God! Her boyfriend must have gotten killed."

"Nooooo!" Lilly screamed, her hands clutching at her head.

Erika had just returned from the library and pushed her way to the front of the crowd. She softly embraced Lilly. Lilly rested her head on her roommate's shoulder and sobbed, her entire upper body shaking as she cried.

"Lilly, what is it? Is it Paul? What's happened?" Erika asked.

Lilly looked into Erika's eyes, tears streaming down her face.

"Paul's missing! He was shot down three days ago—he may have been captured—or worse—oh Erika!" Lilly leaned against her friend and cried. She was inconsolable.

The girls who had swarmed into the hallway gently parted and made a path. With the help of another friend, Erika got Lilly to her feet and guided her back to their room.

Erika made some tea and sat close to Lilly on her bed, rubbing her back. Eventually, Lilly calmed down enough to tell Erika what had happened. She managed to sip at the cup pressed to her lips. She put it gently down on the bedside table before burying herself under the covers.

Then, mercifully, everything went black. She fell into a deep sleep. She was mentally and emotionally drained and physically exhausted.

*   *   *

As promised, her parents drove down from Brookline the next morning to check on her. Lilly didn't attend classes that day. Instead, she spent the day with her parents. They were staying at the Gideon Putnam Hotel, a historic old hotel nestled in the foothills of the Adirondack Mountains and a short drive from Skidmore. She barely noticed her father speaking when he gently suggested that focusing on her coursework would be therapeutic for her.

As they sat on the patio overlooking the Adirondack Mountains, Lilly felt disconnected from the beautiful scenery that surrounded them. It was the weekend, and the hotel was quickly filling up and becoming a gathering spot for tourists, vacationers, and fall foliage peepers. She saw people unloading suitcases and golf clubs from their cars on this beautiful early fall day, smiling and waving as they greeted friends. She felt numb. She felt that she didn't belong here in this place where people had come to relax and enjoy time with their loved ones. She wanted to run away. Far, far away.

Lilly's father tried to be reassuring. She glanced at him across the patio table. Her parents had ordered sandwiches for lunch. Hers remained untouched.

"Lilly, we know this is going to be a difficult time but try to stay positive. Right now, Paul is considered missing in action, and until we hear otherwise, we need to have faith that he's alive and he'll be home again."

Her mother gently rubbed Lilly's arm as she tried to offer words of encouragement.

Her mother spoke to her with tenderness. "Lilly, think about what Paul would want. He would want you to stay focused on your studies and keep the faith. He told you he would be back— we must hold onto hope. We don't know anything for sure yet. Let's save our tears for now."

She knew her parents meant well, but their words felt empty. Meaningless. She also knew that she needed to somehow make them feel like she was going to be ok. They couldn't stay in Saratoga Springs forever and right now she just wanted to go back to her dorm room and sleep the time away. She pretended she felt better and that she would do what they asked her to do—keep busy and remain hopeful.

"Yes, I'm sure Paul would want me to stay in school, keep studying, and stay busy while we wait to hear more."

There was no emotion in her voice as she spoke, but her parents seemed to accept that she was starting to feel a little better and believed that she would show resilience and stay positive.

Her father stood up from the table, grabbed his hat from the bench, and looked out onto the rolling lawn in front of the hotel. He turned to Lilly.

"Let's take a walk around town before we bring you back to

school. It's a beautiful day. A nice long walk in the fresh autumn air will be good for all of us."

By the end of the day, she felt well enough to return to her dorm room, where Erika did her best to comfort her.

The next morning Lilly's parents joined her for breakfast at the school dining hall. She had no appetite but forced herself to eat some toast and a few pieces of fruit. She was slowly dying inside yet didn't want her parents to worry about her. She wanted to make sure they felt ok about leaving to go back home.

Her father was a respected district court judge who rarely missed a day's work; he had already canceled two days' worth of proceedings to come to Saratoga Springs. Always the dutiful daughter, Lilly assured them that she would be all right and forced herself to smile. She hugged them tightly when they dropped her off at the entrance to her dorm.

She stood at the curb waving goodbye as they drove away, but when she turned to her dorm, she felt an indescribable sense of emptiness and profound loss.

If Paul wasn't coming home, she knew her life would never be the same. She felt lost, as if she had just fallen off a cliff and was floating untethered.

*   *   *

The next few days she barely functioned. It was as if the world around her continued to move, but she found herself standing still, lost in disbelief. She felt detached from the world. She attended classes, but it was as if she was merely an observer. She cried herself to sleep each night and started to have nightmares.

A few days after her parents had left to return to Brookline, one nightmare began to haunt her. She woke up in a cold sweat screaming his name.

"Paul! Paul! I'm coming for you!"

Erika jumped out of bed and ran over to where Lilly had suddenly awoken from her sleep.

"Lilly, look at me! It's ok—it's just a dream. You're alright. You're here with me. You're safe."

Lilly turned to look at her friend, who was doing her best to provide comfort and reassure her.

"Oh Erika! It's not a dream—it's a nightmare. And waking up doesn't make it go away! Don't you see? Every day I am living a nightmare. I keep thinking of Paul being lost or hurt or tortured and no one coming to help him. I keep hearing his voice calling out to me. In my dream I'm running to find him in the dark but can never reach him. It's awful."

All that they had shared was in the past. There would be no future together.

She spent most nights talking with Erika, who continued to be supportive and amazingly kind. They sat up talking for hours at a time. Instead of tea, they drank wine, which calmed Lilly's nerves. The conversations were therapeutic for Lilly, but her sense of loss was profound. She began to sink into a deep depression and couldn't focus on her schoolwork.

She would often talk to Erika about how she felt.

"I'll never love any man the way I loved Paul. It was Kismet.

That kind of physical, mental, and emotional connection is rare. Some people never find it. I'll never find that kind of love twice in my lifetime."

Erika seemed to be at a loss for words, and Lilly suspected she agreed but didn't want to say so.

"Just take it one day at a time, Lil. In the meantime, I'm right here if you need me." She turned off the light, and another night slowly passed.

Chapter 8

Time Passes Slowly

D AYS TURNED INTO nights and the weight of Paul's absence pressed upon her.

Lilly had started going home on weekends, taking comfort from being with her parents until she finally decided to leave school and take a break from her classes for a while. Her parents were growing increasingly concerned about her and agreed coming home to Brookline was the right decision.

Her brother Mark often came home on the weekends to check in on her and she spent a lot of time visiting Paul's parents. Their hearts were shattered, but Mr. and Mrs. Fletcher remained optimistic about Paul's chances for survival, even after it was reported that several men in his platoon were confirmed KIA, killed in action, and that it was likely Paul was among them. They refused to accept the Gold Star the marines had delivered to their home a few days before Lilly's last visit. They refused to believe that Paul wasn't coming home. Lilly thought it was a coping mechanism and tried to be upbeat and positive when they shared this latest update.

She would often feel a temporary renewed sense of hope after visiting with them. Surely Paul wasn't dead. *Wouldn't she feel it somehow if he was?* The marines didn't know everything. Maybe they were wrong to presume Paul was dead.

But as the days turned into weeks, with no additional information or news of his whereabouts, her hope began to fade. She lost faith and started to fear the worst. While initially it was hard for her to believe that he was dead, it had now become even harder for her to imagine that he was alive. She watched the news reports every day. She heard the statistics and saw the Chinook helicopters that were shot down over the jungle and rice paddies in Vietnam. Every day she saw the coffins draped in American flags that returned home and were laid to rest in Arlington National Cemetery. She believed it was only a matter of time before Paul was one of them. They just hadn't found him yet, so closure alluded all of them.

Lilly struggled to get up each day and carry on. She received support from lots of family and close friends, including, of all people, Roger Wentworth.

He called her immediately after learning about Paul's disappearance and arranged to visit her when she moved back to Brookline.

At first his concern surprised her, and then she remembered what Paul had said about him.

"Underneath his bravado and sometimes bad behavior is a really nice guy."

During the next several weeks, she and Roger shared stories about Paul, as if talking about him would somehow keep him alive. Eventually, their conversation strayed to other topics. Roger visited her most weekends. He was living in Cambridge and attending Harvard Law School, so was only about twenty minutes away from the Conroy's house in Brookline. They lived in a traditional brick colonial home with four bedrooms, three bathrooms, and a lovely flower garden overlooking a pond near the Brookline reservoir.

Lilly's parents were grateful for his visits and often thanked him by inviting him to stay for dinner. They appreciated his care and concern. Many of Lilly's other friends were away at school and Roger had quickly become a steady source of comfort and support during a very difficult time.

One evening Roger asked Lilly to go for a walk around the reservoir after dinner.

"Lilly, I miss Paul more than you probably realize. He was my best friend. Somehow spending time with you and talking about him makes me feel better."

"You've been a good friend, Roger. Between you and my roommate at Skidmore, I don't know how I would have gotten through this time without your visits. It's been a good distraction."

Roger abruptly stopped walking and turned to face her. A bitter November wind was blowing, and it was getting cold. He rubbed his hands together to keep them warm as he began to speak.

"Paul was my best friend, Lilly. He would want me to take

care of you. I have something to ask you, Lilly. Something very important."

"What is it?" Lilly asked.

"I know that Paul asked you to marry him, Lilly. He told me before he shipped out to Fort Bragg. He told me he was planning to buy you a real ring when he returned. I know he wanted you to have the most beautiful ring he could afford to buy when he got back. I want to be here for you, Lilly. I want to take care of you the way Paul would have taken care of you. He wouldn't want you to be alone. He wouldn't want you to go on grieving for him and to be sad forever. He loved you, Lilly, and I know he would want you to find happiness again."

Lilly had suspected that Roger was falling in love with her. He went on to promise that he would commit his whole life to making her happy because that is what Paul would have wanted but, she knew in fact, it was what *Roger* wanted.

He fell down on one knee and officially proposed to her with a beautiful diamond ring.

"This is the ring I know Paul would have wanted you to have. Will you marry me, Lilly? So that I can do what I know Paul would want me to do? I promise to take care of you and love you for the rest of my life."

She was stunned. It had only been a few short months since Paul disappeared. Yet she convinced herself that marrying Roger was the right thing to do. She didn't believe Paul was coming home. She clung to each passing day hoping for some clarity, or a vision for the future besides the constant darkness and the utterly profound feeling of emptiness in her heart. The future she had dreamed about with Paul was now in the past. Gone forever.

Roger understood her grief.

They married at his parents' home the following month, just before the holidays.

It was a small wedding, limited to close friends and family who understood that both Lilly and Roger were still grieving Paul's loss.

Many of them also looked at Roger as a hero, providing loving support and kindness during some of Lilly's darkest days. Lilly's parents found comfort knowing that Roger would take good care of Lilly.

Even Paul's parents didn't want to see her sad anymore. It added to their heartache and they cared about her too much to see her unhappy day after day. They too were worried about her deepening depression.

The only one who dared to ask Lilly if she was doing the right thing on the day of her wedding was Erika. They were upstairs in the Wentworth's master bedroom suite. Erika was going to be Lilly's Maid of Honor and was helping her get ready. The wedding would be simple, and Lilly chose to wear a cream knee-length chiffon dress. Nothing too fancy. No veil or lacy train.

Erika had become Lilly's confidante when Paul went missing and she wasn't really sure she understood why she was rushing into a marriage with Roger Wentworth.

As she looked in the full-length mirror standing by Lilly's side and admiring her dress, Erika gathered up the courage to ask what only a true friend would ask a bride on her wedding day.

"Lilly, are you sure this is the right thing to do? Maybe you should wait a little longer before getting married. It all seems to be happening so fast. I know how much you loved Paul and I think you're still grieving. I know Roger has been good to you—but running into his arms and getting married isn't going to make your sadness go away, at least not right now. It takes time, Lilly. Why are you rushing into this?"

Lilly slowly turned to face her friend and replied gently. She knew Erika was only looking out for her best interests. Erika knew her deepest thoughts. She understood Lilly's feelings like no one else could during the past few months.

Lilly spoke softly. "Erika, don't you see it doesn't really matter? Losing Paul meant losing the only future I had ever dreamed about. I will never love anyone the way I loved Paul, but I can't go on like this. Roger is giving me a path forward. He's been a lifeline during a time when I was drowning in sadness. I need a path forward, Erika. This is the path I've chosen."

Erika began to question her once again "But Lilly do you really think this is . . ."

Lilly interrupted her friend. "And there's something else that you should know. I'm pregnant."

Erika stood silently. She suddenly understood. They never spoke of it again—not until Lilly filed for divorce almost twenty years later.

Chapter 9

The Phone Call

Mattapoisett
July 4, 1990

LILLY'S ARMS WERE filled with groceries from the Mattapoisett Market as she made her way onto the porch and fumbled to open the front door of the beach house. Today was her thirty-ninth birthday, a typical hot July day, and she looked forward to taking a quick swim.

She placed the groceries on the table and was in the middle of putting them away when the kitchen phone began to ring. She turned to pick up the receiver of the old yellow rotary wall phone her parents had never updated. It still had their old phone number from the sixties typed on the dial pad—five-five-four-two-seven. No area code, no prefix, just the local line. Phone service was only activated during the summer months when the house was occupied and there had never been a real need to update the phone during all these years.

"Lilly, you're not going to believe it!" Charlotte's voice

bellowed through the phone. Lilly was grateful the two of them had rekindled their friendship over the past few weeks. Charlotte had been Mark's girlfriend for a short time, and she and Lilly had remained friends.

Charlotte and her husband, Jack Farris, had built a house near the yacht club. It felt good to reconnect during the past few weeks—spending time with her brought back fond childhood memories of fun times. Charlotte also had a son Charlie who was the same age as John and the two had become sailing buddies over the past few weeks.

Lilly couldn't imagine why Charlotte was so excited. "Charlotte, slow down. What is it? Is everything all right?" She continued to unload the groceries as she talked on the phone— its long cord wrapped around her waist as Lilly worked her way back and forth from the table to the refrigerator with her groceries.

"More than all right. You're not going to believe it!"

"OK, Charlotte. You said that twice already. What is it that I'm not going to believe? Are you pregnant again?" At forty, Charlotte was the mother of four children under the age of twelve, the youngest being only four.

Charlotte laughed out loud. "Are you kidding? Of course not! That door is closed—four is enough for me!"

"Well, what is it, then?" Lilly was starting to get annoyed. She wanted to finish putting away the groceries and head to the beach. Kate was returning from Greece this afternoon, and Lilly had a lot to get done before the annual clambake down at the yacht club.

"I think you should sit down."

Lilly let out a sigh—she was losing her patience and feeling exasperated. Charlotte definitely had a flair for the dramatic—but Lilly dutifully sat on one of the yellow Formica chairs that matched the old kitchen table.

"All right, I'm sitting down. You have my full attention. Now, what is it?"

"You know this year's clambake is in conjunction with Doctors Without Borders, right?"

"Yes, you mentioned that to me." Each year's Fourth of July clambake raised money for a hospital charity or local non-profit organization.

"Well, guess who'll be speaking tonight and accepting the donation?"

Lilly had little time for gossip and was getting annoyed. She had to get John down to the pier in time for the regatta at ten, finish unloading the groceries, and be at Logan Airport in time to meet Kate's plane at three o'clock.

"I don't know, Charlotte. Who is it? Just tell me, please! I have a lot to do today."

"Paul Fletcher."

The receiver slipped out of Lilly's hand and hit the floor with a thud. She actually felt the color drain from her face. Her hands began to tremble.

A day hadn't gone by over the past twenty years that she hadn't thought of him. All through her marriage her heart had longed for him. There were nights when she still cried over losing him.

"Charlotte, what are you talking about?" Lilly demanded when she retrieved the receiver. "This isn't funny. Paul is dead, and you know it."

Charlotte's voice softened. "Lilly, didn't anyone ever tell you what happened to Paul?"

"What do you mean?" Her heart suddenly began to flutter. She felt hot and cold at the same time. She could barely say the words.

"He's *alive?*"

Seconds ticked by before Charlotte replied. "Yes—alive and looking quite well! I know it's a sensitive topic and figured that if you wanted to talk about Paul, you'd be the one to broach the subject. I just assumed you knew he had come back all those years ago. It's been such a long time and we all moved on. You got married, had kids. It wasn't until this morning that I found out he was here. I suddenly realized you should know that he's back. I didn't want you to be surprised or possibly even shocked when he walked in tonight."

Lilly's lips trembled as she tried to speak.

"He's here in Mattapoisett? After all these years? Wha-what happened to him?"

Charlotte spoke in a soft and soothing tone. "Didn't anyone ever tell you? He was held as a prisoner of war . . . for five years. He wasn't released until the withdrawal from Vietnam in 1973."

"*What?!*" Lilly screamed into the phone.

"Didn't Roger ever tell you? He must have known about it. Paul must have tried to call or write. He and Roger were so close. Didn't your parents ever say anything about it? Paul must have tried to reach you even if you . . . even if you were just high school sweethearts . . ."

She trailed off, but Lilly knew what she was about to say. *Even if you married his best friend.*

"I'm so sorry, Lilly. I thought you knew, but of course by the time Paul was released you were married to Roger and had started a family. I'm sure reuniting with Paul after all those years would have been out of the question. We all knew that Paul must have just accepted the fact that you had gone on with your life."

Charlotte's voice took on a defensive edge. "It's been over fifteen years since he came back from Vietnam. His parents sold their house here, but his return did make the Boston news. I know you were living in New York by then, but surely your parents must have told you . . ."

Tears ran down Lilly's cheeks. She realized that her parents, as well as Roger, must have known Paul was alive but hadn't told her. Her mind raced with conflicting ideas as to why they wouldn't have told her. She thought about how much her parents loved her—and their grandchildren. It had been years since Paul was MIA. Most everyone had given up hope that he would ever return. Even the Fletchers had sold their home in Mattapoisett and moved to Maine to escape the memories. Her parents probably felt nothing good would come of her knowing Paul was alive.

Her mind quickly turned to Roger. He had always known that her heart belonged to Paul . . . his reasons for not telling her were purely selfish. How different her life would have been if she'd only known the truth.

Her mind was quickly becoming a jumbled mess of thoughts. She started to feel an immediate sense of shock and confusion.

She wanted her friend to repeat the words. Paul wasn't dead. Paul was in Mattapoisett.

Her heart began to ache at the thought of him returning home and finding out she hadn't waited for him. She had broken the promise they made to each other all those years ago.

She shook her head in disbelief. Paul wasn't killed in action—he'd been held prisoner for five long years. Her thoughts turned to him. *My darling Paul. What he must have gone through . . .*

Charlotte kept talking, but her words barely registered as Lilly became absorbed once again in various "what-if" scenarios.

Charlotte carried on. "Anyways, I just saw him this morning leaving the hotel for a walk on the beach. He looks fantastic! A little older, of course, and his face is a bit worn—but he still has that incredible smile and those beautiful blue eyes. He's as handsome as ever. He said this is his first time back in Mattapoisett since he left for Vietnam."

Lilly was barely listening. She thought about Paul's parents. The Fletchers had sold their cottage and moved to Maine to get away from their memories and all the familiar places that reminded them of their missing son. They must have been crying tears of joy the day he came home!

"He told me he travels most of the time," Charlotte kept talking at a dizzying pace, "helping to bring vaccines to third world countries. He just got back from Ethiopia. And, apparently, he's never been married! Of course, I asked, and he told me that all the travel makes it difficult for him to sustain a serious relationship and he doesn't know if he'll ever settle down. Which means . . . the door just opened for you to reconnect with him!"

Lilly's mind shifted to the words she had just heard. She suddenly felt an overwhelming curiosity to know more. "Did he ask about me?"

"I asked if he knew you'd married Roger. I thought I saw him wince. He said yes, he knew. His parents told him when he arrived home. I guess that's why he never contacted you. A part of me thinks that may be why he travels all the time—he doesn't seem to really have a home base, from what he told me. I had to run back to the house and tell you. I think it's fate. You're both here again for the first time in twenty years, and you're both single and available!" Charlotte paused, breathless. "Aren't you excited about seeing him again?"

Lilly let out a breath. She was going to see Paul, again? After all these years? It felt surreal, like she was living a dream, or suddenly waking up from a nightmare and wondering what was real and what was imagined.

"Lilly, are you there? What time will you be at the clambake? How about six-thirty? And how about wearing that new black dress you bought the other day when we were at the Cape Cod Mall—that will get his attention! What better way to celebrate your birthday—it's going to be a great night! Happy birthday!"

Lilly, still holding the receiver, stared at nothing.

"Lilly, are you still there?" Charlotte pressed.

Lilly cleared her throat and spoke in a voice that sounded strangely detached to her own ears. "This is a lot to absorb right now, but yes, of course, it will be nice to see Paul again. I'll meet you there at seven. I don't think I can make it by six-thirty. I have a lot to do today."

"Goodbye, Charlotte."

She went up to her bedroom and pulled out the old letters wrapped in blue ribbon from the protective zip pouch in her purse. She had carried these letters with her for over twenty years. She sat on the bed and opened the tear-stained envelope postmarked September 30, 1969. It was the last letter she received from him.

She read it for what must have been the millionth time. By the time she put it away, her vision was blurred with tears. That letter had brought her both joy and pain since the day it had been delivered, a week after Paul went missing. Time and time again she told herself she needed to let it go . . . but she couldn't bring herself to do it. Letting go of the letter meant letting go of him. Of his thoughts, his words, his love for her.

She reflected on the past. Her decision to marry Roger seemed like the best thing to do. He represented stability at a time when her life was spinning out of control.

But throughout her marriage she carried a little piece of Paul with her every day.

She only had to look at her beautiful daughter to be reminded of him—and to feel the joy, love, longing, and the sweet connection to Paul's bittersweet presence.

Kate shared her father's steel-blue eyes.

Chapter 10

The Yacht Club

THE REST OF the day seemed long, despite being busy. Lilly watched John sail in his first regatta but felt distracted. While his team didn't win, the smile on his face as he rounded the last race marker and sailed for the finish line made her smile. His grandfather and uncle would be proud. He wasn't among the top finishers, but nor was he last, which wasn't bad for a new sailor!

After the race she and John drove to the airport and welcomed Kate home with lunch at the Mattapoisett Inn and then dessert at Gulf Hill for ice cream. It had changed hands over the years, but still looked and tasted much the same. Kate was excited to be back home, spending time with her mother and brother in Mattapoisett and eager to explore.

Lilly was thrilled to have Kate back but found herself frequently checking her watch in spite of her happiness. She showered and changed as soon as they got home from the airport.

She felt anxious, nervous, sad, and happy all at the same time as she reflected on the phone call with Charlotte earlier that day. She was still walking around the house in disbelief.

As she looked at herself in the mirror upstairs, she hoped Charlotte was right and that her little black cocktail dress hid her imperfections.

"What would Paul think when he saw her?" she wondered. She had a slight tan and a few summer freckles on her face, which added a healthy glow.

It had been so long! She wondered if she had, in fact, aged well. The last time he saw her she was a teenager. It was a lifetime ago. Yet it felt like she had suddenly slipped back in time. It was her birthday, and she felt the same way she did all those years ago when he arrived at the house with the beautiful bouquet of flowers and gave her the ring after the bonfire. She still had that ring—she kept it in the same blue box he had given her that night.

Fully dressed, she headed downstairs, and poured herself a glass of white wine in the kitchen. Kate was tired after her cross-Atlantic flight and was in the kitchen pouring a glass of lemonade.

"Kate, would you mind watching John tonight? I was planning to go to the yacht club for the July Fourth clambake to meet up with some old friends."

"That sounds like fun! Sure, I'll watch John. I'm tired and don't really have any plans to do anything. We can stay in and watch TV. I'll see what games we have here. Maybe I'll teach John how to play gin rummy."

She gave Lilly a little kiss on the cheek—something she didn't do very often these days.

She stepped back and admired Lilly's dress. "You look great, Mom! Have fun tonight!" Kate turned and headed back upstairs to bring John his lemonade.

As she watched Kate walk away, part of Lilly felt at peace knowing she would be sleeping under the same roof with both her children again. She had missed Kate terribly and was glad she was home.

When she looked at the kitchen clock, she couldn't believe it was finally 6:45 p.m. She felt a flutter in her stomach. She quickly finished her last sip of wine, took a deep breath, and set off down the dirt road toward the Bitter End Yacht Club.

A sudden sense of freedom and excitement washed over her as she walked down the road. She hadn't felt like this in a very long time.

* * *

As she neared the club, she saw Charlotte waving enthusiastically from the porch that overlooked the ocean. Lilly recognized Charlotte's royal blue sleeveless cocktail dress. They had bought it in Hyannis when they were shopping together. The dress complimented Charlotte's petite frame and looked stunning against her shoulder-length red hair.

In the brief time Lilly had been back in town, Charlotte had proven herself to be a warm and caring friend. Charlotte had been happily married for over fifteen years. Lilly couldn't help feeling a little envious that her own life had not turned out as smoothly.

As Lilly started across the lawn, she looked out to Buzzards Bay. It was a beautiful evening, still hot, but the warm summer breeze made it bearable. The water was still, and the boats reflected against the water as the sun began to set.

"I'm so glad to see you!" Charlotte ran over and gave Lilly a big hug.

"Part of me thought you might change your mind about coming."

Lilly tried to smile. "I almost turned around at least three times on the way here. I'm so nervous, Charlotte. Seeing Paul again after all these years . . . look at my palms! I'm sweating— or maybe it's a hot flash. I honestly don't know what I'm going to say when I see him." She drew in a deep breath. "Is he here yet? Have you seen him?"

"Yes, but I didn't tell him you were coming," Charlotte said. "He's inside at the bar having a few drinks with Jack and the others. I'm sure he'll be thrilled to see you, Lilly. Don't worry."

As they approached the club's front entrance, the music got louder. Lilly noted the good turnout—about seventy-five people had spilled out onto the porch—and she heard the boisterous laughter drifting through the windows.

The July Fourth holiday was like a high school reunion, with everyone spending the entire week at their summer cottages and reconnecting with friends and neighbors. Unlike Memorial Day weekend, when it tended to be cooler, the summer season was in full swing in July. But while some people were reconnecting with their neighbors for the first time in nearly a year, for Paul and Lilly it had been much longer than that . . .

Her old childhood friend Sarah came running over and gave her a big hug.

"Lilly, it's so nice to see you! It's been years—I'm so glad you're here. We just ordered a round of drinks. Come with me—everyone's at the bar."

Lilly hesitated but before she knew it, Sarah had grabbed her hand and was leading her over to where their friends had gathered, talking and laughing. She was vaguely aware and barely recognized some other old friends, including Sarah's husband, James, who'd also spent his childhood summers in Mattapoisett; and Charlotte's husband, Jack, who'd grown up in Rhode Island. Like James and the other husbands, Jack worked in the city during the week and came out to Mattapoisett on the weekends. But her gaze immediately went to the man sitting just a few feet away at the bar and staring directly at her.

Sarah spoke loudly over the chatter and laughter. "Lilly is here, everyone! Doesn't she look fabulous? Let's order her a drink and make a toast to old times!"

Everyone said hello, with a few coming over to greet her with hugs and kisses. And before she knew it, she had a vodka martini in her hand, and everyone was raising their glass. Lilly felt detached from the party unfolding around her.

Her eyes were locked on him.

He continued to stare at her.

The crisp, light blue Oxford he wore accentuated his slate-blue eyes.

At forty-three, he looked incredible. His sandy brown hair was now accentuated with a few strands of gray that the light caught, mostly at the temples; his face was deeply tanned, almost weatherworn. *But he was still incredibly handsome,* Lilly thought to herself. He looked as fit and trim as the football player and all-star hockey player he'd been in high school.

He stood and raised his glass, his eyes never leaving her.

"To old friends and good times!" Sarah shouted over the music.

Paul kept staring, as if transfixed, and then slowly smiled as he lowered his glass to the bar and began moving toward her.

Lilly, too, was unable to look away. She immediately felt the physical attraction that had first brought them together all those years ago. Her heart began to race. She felt that old familiar flutter in her stomach. It all felt so surreal, it made her a little lightheaded. Like an impossible dream come true, and after living through the nightmare of losing him so long ago, she never wanted this dream of seeing him again to end.

He was getting closer by the second, their eyes locked, they continued staring at each other as he came closer. His clear blue eyes always drew her in, like the sky on a cloudless summer day. The gray in his hair made him look distinguished and even more attractive. She promptly forgot all that was happening around her; the laughter and music suddenly drifted away.

Then, incredibly, there he was, after all these years. Standing just inches away from her.

He leaned in and kissed her cheek. His lips were moist and warm as they lightly grazed her cheek. She felt his breath as he softly whispered, "Hello, Lilly," in her ear.

Her eyes closed for a moment as she smelled his cologne.

Paul took a step back and looked at her admiringly. "It's good to see you again. You look beautiful."

Lilly gulped. She wanted to touch him, to reach back out and hug him, but didn't dare. She'd become conscious of the curious stares of her childhood friends.

She felt her hands trembling as she held on tight to the glass in her hand and tried not to spill it as she thought about what to say.

She managed a faint smile as she spoke. "Hello, Paul. It's been a long time." Her voice cracked slightly. She wasn't sure what to say next as they stood staring but was saved by an announcement asking everyone to take their seats so dinner could be served.

She'd almost forgotten about the fundraiser that night for Doctors without Borders. That was, after all, the reason he was here.

Charlotte appeared at her side.

"Come on, you two. You're sitting at our table near the stage."

The room was filling up as she and Paul followed Charlotte to the table. Lilly inadvertently bumped against him when she stepped back to let someone pass. She felt a sudden rush from the physical connection.

"*Excuse* me!"

He smiled and took her elbow, guiding her through the mass of people.

She wondered if he was watching her and suddenly felt very self-conscious. Like the gentleman he was, he pulled her chair out for her, and she sat down.

As dinner was served, talk came easy to this group of mostly old friends. They updated each other on their jobs, their kids, and the health of their aging parents. When asked what was new in her life, Lilly hesitated, not sure what to say but decided to be forthright.

"Well, I'm sure most of you know I'm divorced." She was certain Charlotte had already shared this news, but she didn't feel comfortable going into more detail with Paul at the table.

"I have two children, a nineteen-year-old daughter, Kate, who's a sophomore at NYU, and an eleven-year-old son, John, who's in middle school. We live in upstate New York, but I thought it would be nice for us to spend a special summer here in Mattapoisett after all these years. It's been a long time."

"Yes, Lilly finally got rid of that loser in her life, otherwise known as Roger Wentworth," Charlotte suddenly blurted out.

"Let's raise our glasses to her and her new status as a single woman!"

Everyone smiled and raised their glasses.

"I always knew you were too good for him," Sarah said. "I just wish you had done it sooner."

Lilly felt very uncomfortable and glanced at Paul. His puzzled expression told her that he may not have been aware of her divorce. She wished with all her heart that someone would change the subject. Charlotte had obviously had too much to drink. She was slurring her words and talking loudly as she sipped what was clearly not her first or second glass of wine.

Sarah was the first one to speak. "I didn't realize your daughter was in college. You and Roger didn't waste any time, did you?"

"Sarah," Charlotte said, her voice holding a warning.

Everyone at the table looked uncomfortable, and Lilly, not daring to look at Paul, gave Charlotte a desperate look.

Just then Charlie Peck, Commandant of the Yacht Club, cleared his throat.

"Paul, why don't we head over to the stage and check the sound system?"

Paul placed his drink on the table. "Sure." He turned to face his friends seated at the table. "Excuse us."

While the table conversation turned to summer vacation plans, Lilly's eyes strayed to Paul and Charlie, who had gone to the podium and tested the microphone. He was shaking hands and talking with people near the stage, making no effort to return to the table.

As she watched him mingling with the crowd it struck her that he was somewhat of a local celebrity tonight. But who could blame everyone for treating him that way. He had served in Vietnam, was a prisoner of war, had finally returned home, and was helping to raise thousands of dollars for a worthy cause.

Lilly suddenly felt inferior and started to doubt whether he had thought about her at all over the years.

By the time they returned to the table, dessert was being served.

"How are you?" Lilly asked Paul as he began to sit down. She was speaking softly so no one else could hear.

"I'm fine." He sounded almost nonchalant.

After dessert, Charlie and Paul once again went to the podium "Good evening, everyone!" Charlie greeted the crowd, his voice amplified by the microphone. Most of the attendees ignored him and continued talking, while a few turned their chairs to face the stage. By now, most of the crowd was feeling no pain. Charlotte and some others began tapping their silverware against their water glasses to get the attention of the slightly inebriated audience.

"Thank you," Charlie said when he had finally grabbed the crowd's attention. He introduced himself and then presented the chairwoman, his wife, Stephanie, who addressed the group.

"As you know, each year we host this annual event to benefit a specific charity. I want to thank you all for contributing this year. We sold nearly three hundred tickets and raised over ten thousand dollars, which will be donated to Doctors Without Borders for global health and vaccines for underserved patients as part of their partnership with Massachusetts General Hospital."

Her words were met with applause and cheers.

"I have the honor of introducing tonight's special guest speaker. Many of you here tonight remember him from the summers he spent here in Mattapoisett. This is the first time Dr. Fletcher has visited Mattapoisett since he left for Vietnam over twenty years ago. He has dedicated his life to helping provide vaccines to prevent illnesses and epidemics in underdeveloped countries." She paused. "Ladies and gentlemen, please join me in welcoming our very own Dr. Paul Fletcher of Doctors Without Borders." She and Charlie led the applause, which swelled as Paul stepped in front of the microphone.

Lilly clapped vigorously, her eyes filling with tears. How wonderful that Paul wasn't lying in a grave, but very much alive! It was so good to see him again. He looked vibrant and healthy as he took to the stage. He had given so much, and still had so much to give . . . her thoughts began to wander.

She began to wonder about his personal life as she sat and admired all that he had done over the past twenty years. Charlotte had said he never married, but was he involved with someone, even casually?

He waved to the audience, then gestured for them to stop applauding and to be seated as many stood to welcome him. "Thank you so much for the warm welcome. It feels good to be back among so many special friends. I've enjoyed taking a trip down memory lane today here in Mattapoisett. Some things never change, and the love and support of good friends is one of them."

Lilly wondered if he considered her to be one of the "good friends" he spoke of—even after all these years. It had been so long that she wondered what their past meant to him now. She'd never stopped loving him, a fact she feared Roger had suspected throughout their marriage. Hardly a day went by when she didn't think of Paul and wish things could have been different. *Did he feel the same way? Had he even thought of her at all?* The questions swirled in her head, and she couldn't stop wondering what he was thinking, especially after seeing her tonight. It was the first time in twenty years that they stood together in the same room.

She barely heard the remainder of Paul's presentation.

Chapter 11

The Dance

C HARLIE PECK RETOOK the podium, acknowledged Paul, and announced that it was time to start dancing! Paul was stopped by several attendees as he made his way back to the table against the backdrop of the party that was unfolding. The deejay kicked things off with an old song—an Elvis Presley cover of the classic love song *Unchained Melody*.

It was the same song they had danced to the last night they were together, although back then it was the Righteous Brothers' version. *Would Paul remember? Or was she alone in thinking back to that summer night twenty years ago?*

She met his gaze as he approached the table. He held out his hand as he drew nearer to where she sat. He stood before her; his arm extended in silent invitation.

"May I have this dance?"

She got up, carelessly tossing her napkin on the table as she placed her hand in his. Their eyes met and held for a moment, and then he led her to the dance floor.

The lights were low, and several couples were already dancing, but as Paul's arm went around her waist and drew her close, Lilly felt as if they were the only two people in the room.

They didn't speak, just moved in time to the music. Lilly allowed herself the luxury of leaning her head on his shoulder and reveled in the feel of the firm, steady beat of his heart.

The song said it all.

I've hungered for your touch for such a long, long time.

Lonely rivers cry, wait for me, wait for me.

Darling, wait for me.

I'll be coming home.

When the music ended, she slowly looked up and into his eyes. It was as if the past two decades had suddenly melted away.

Still holding her close, he softly whispered in her ear, answering the question she dared not ask. "I remember this song, Lilly."

Then he led her back to the table and pulled out her chair for her and thanked her for the dance.

Lilly felt overcome with joy. Somehow, she knew that he'd never forgotten her. She never thought she would see him in this life again, much less dance with him. She looked up at him with a smile. She expected him to sit beside her at the table so they could talk, but instead he turned to James, who was standing nearby.

"How about a round of drinks for the table on me, James? I'd like to thank everyone for their generosity."

"Sounds good to me! Let's hit the bar."

Paul took a moment to confirm what everyone was drinking before walking away with James, much to Lilly's disappointment.

Within a few minutes they returned, James carrying a tray of cold beverages. Paul casually handed her a glass of white wine. He looked at her momentarily, and she thought this was the moment they would break off into a private conversation—but when he sat next to her, he leaned forward and started to chat with Charlotte.

She listened to the chatter for what felt like an eternity, feeling morose. *So that's it—after all these years he has no desire to reconnect or talk about what happened in Vietnam or ask why I married Roger, or . . .* The list went on and on. She had so many questions and wanted to know so much about his time as a prisoner of war.

She wanted to explain how she felt when she learned he'd gone missing . . . how sad, depressed, and utterly hopeless she felt assuming he was never coming back.

But he didn't seem to care.

Just a dance—a brief trip down memory lane and nothing more. She could barely manage to sit still. Paul seemed to want to talk to everyone but her. It suddenly became too much. She couldn't stay there another minute.

She quickly picked up her purse and left the room without looking back. Had she turned around, she would have seen that Paul never took his eyes off her until she slipped out into the darkness of that warm summer night.

She walked fast, eager to get home. She didn't even know

how long he was staying in Mattapoisett. Perhaps he was leaving in the morning to fly off to some third world country.

She opened the back door to the cottage, walked through the kitchen, and forced herself to sound cheerful as she checked in on Kate, who was lounging on the sofa, a bowl of popcorn on the coffee table and her ear glued to the phone. Lilly made a gesture feigning sleep to indicate she was going to bed before blowing Kate a kiss and climbing the stairs to her room. She felt emotionally drained and mentally exhausted.

The evening had begun with so much anticipation and hope. She had started to think that after all these years they would find themselves together again. Instead, the night ended with crushing disappointment and a sense of longing. She feared they might never see each other again and had no idea if he would be staying for a few days or flying out this morning.

Maybe it's for the best, she thought. She had to consider her daughter. Paul's return meant that she was keeping a huge secret from him. She struggled thinking about how and when she should tell him that they had a daughter together. And what about Kate? Telling Paul the secret she had kept for all these years meant telling Kate the truth. And how would Kate feel once she found out that the person she knew as her father was merely a stand-in for the real man? She worried Kate would feel betrayed. The thought of doing anything to jeopardize her relationship with her only daughter was impossible to bear.

Maybe the best thing she could do was to let sleeping dogs lie, she thought to herself.

She pulled down the summer quilt, slowly got into bed,

and wrapped herself in the sheets without even bothering to get undressed. She could still smell his cologne on her dress. Somehow it offered her comfort, as if he was with her and still holding her close.

She replayed the night over and over again in her mind before finally drifting off to sleep.

Chapter 12

The Morning After

S HE AWOKE TO the sound of the phone ringing beside her bed. The morning sun streamed through the window and the birds were chirping outside. She reached for the phone on the nightstand and looked over at the alarm clock. It was 8:00 a.m.

She felt groggy and for a brief moment wondered if the night before had been a dream.

Had she really seen him last night? Had they danced together?

"Good morning, Lilly!" Charlotte greeted, sounding way too chipper for this early in the morning, but of course she had little ones at home and was up early. Lilly desperately needed a cup of coffee. Perhaps she should have let the call go unanswered. It was too early in the morning for a deep conversation with Charlotte about last night.

She sat up in bed and swept her hair back behind her ears. Suppressing a sigh, she replied, "Hello, Charlotte, how are you this morning?"

"I'm doing great! We had so much fun last night! But I was worried about you, leaving so early and without saying goodbye? Are you OK? None of us even realized you'd left until the party broke up and we were all saying goodbyes. I asked Paul if he knew where you were, and he said he saw you slip out earlier in the evening. What happened?"

"I wanted to talk to him, but he didn't seem interested in talking to me. I found myself taking a long walk down memory lane after we danced together, and it just got to be too much. I didn't mean to be rude, but I had to get out of there. I was beginning to feel like I was having an anxiety attack." Lilly sighed. "It's probably for the best. Sometimes the past is better left there."

"I don't know about that, but I'm glad you're OK. And I had another reason for calling. Jack and I decided to have a few close friends over tonight for a cookout. We'll grill a few steaks, pour some wine, and just enjoy each other's company. Can you come? Seven o'clock?"

"Thanks for the invite, Charlotte. I'm not sure I'm up for it, though. I've got a bit of a headache." Lilly knew the "close friends" Charlotte referred to included Paul, and she didn't know if she could handle seeing him again, not after he'd been so indifferent last night.

She was conflicted. On the one hand, she wanted him to know that she still cared for him, that she never stopped loving him, that she had only married Roger out of desperation after convincing herself that Paul would never be coming back. Yet, another part of her felt maybe it was best to just leave the pain, heartache, and sadness in the past.

A battle was going on between her head and her heart. She desperately needed Paul to understand . . . wanted him to know she'd never stopped loving him, that marrying Roger hadn't lessened her feelings for him. Sure, in the early years she was able to find happiness with Roger as they focused on raising a family. She was grateful for his support and enjoyed making a home for them and being a mother to Kate and John . . . but there was always something missing.

She wished she could tell Paul the real reason she'd married Roger . . . the secret she'd hidden from everyone except Roger and Erika for the past twenty-one years.

It would be a struggle to see him again and not tell him he was a father, but she knew in her heart that keeping it from Paul would be wrong. He had the right to know. Her mind raced with memories of the milestones in Kate's life . . . all the years Paul had missed.

Hearing Charlotte say Paul's name jolted Lilly back to the present—and back to their phone conversation.

"Did you hear me, Lilly? Lilly? Are you there?"

"I'm here. What did you just say about Paul?"

"I said that I invited Paul to join us."

"I told him I'd invite you too," Charlotte added.

Lilly perked up. "You told him I was coming too? What did he say?"

"He didn't offer a direct response to that. He just said he was looking forward to spending some more time with all of us. So, I think you should rest up and plan to be at my house at seven," Charlotte replied.

In a gentle tone she added, "Lilly, I know how much you loved Paul. I always thought you two would get married, have kids, and live happily ever after when he came back from Vietnam. I know that didn't happen, but now the two of you have a second chance. You're single, and so is he. It's a golden opportunity to turn the page and start over again. Start a new chapter, Lilly. You deserve it—and so does he. You've both been through so much. Don't let this chance slip away." She paused briefly before asking Lilly one more time, "So, you'll come tonight?"

Lilly nodded, even though her friend couldn't see her. She'd made up her mind to go. "Yes, Charlotte, I'll be there."

"I think it'll be good for you two to spend some time together. It had to be rough on Paul to learn that you married his best friend, or former best friend, but I did tell him when I saw him at the beach today that you were shocked when I told you he was going to be the guest speaker. He got a thoughtful look on his face and nodded his head slowly. I think he knew that Roger and your parents never told you when he returned all those years ago."

For once Lilly felt grateful for Charlotte's sometimes intrusive behavior—she always had good intentions but sometimes said too much. So at least Paul knew that much, Lilly thought. *It probably didn't surprise him that I slipped out last night.*

"I told him that Roger had become an alcoholic and that he

was cheating on you. He seemed angry to hear that and asked how long ago your marriage ended. I told him it just became final two months ago."

"Did he say anything else?" Lilly found herself holding her breath.

Charlotte continued, "He told me that after Vietnam he needed to find a purpose, and that helping people who struggled to receive medical care brought meaning to his life. I'm surprised he never got married—or had any children—he's too handsome and nice to be left alone! But maybe it's fate. You came here to start over, Lilly. This could be the path you're meant to follow."

Lilly's lips curved into a smile. Charlotte was certainly enjoying playing matchmaker. "OK, Charlotte. I'll see you at seven. I'll bring some dessert and a bottle of wine!"

She hung up the phone, took a deep breath, and headed downstairs to make breakfast for Kate so they could talk before John came home. Lilly wanted to spend time with her this morning and hear more about her summer abroad and her new boyfriend.

Then she started to think again about What Paul's return meant for Kate . . . if she told Paul, she'd have to tell her daughter.

Lilly headed to the kitchen to make a pot of coffee. She heard Kate coming down the stairs and pushed those thoughts out of her head. She needed to stay focused on what she knew she wanted to say to Paul. She could figure out the best way to handle the issue with Kate later.

Chapter 13

The Dinner Party

WHEN LILLY ARRIVED at Charlotte's later that evening, she heard laughter and music coming from the back patio. Lilly walked around the side of the cottage that faced the bay and saw Charlotte, Jack, Sarah, and James sitting in lawn chairs around a fire. Paul stood in front of the minibar Charlotte had set up in a corner, pouring himself a drink. He had his back toward her, but she recognized him right away.

It was a cool night. The breeze off the ocean had dropped the temperature into the sixties. Lilly wore a white cotton sweater over a black tank top, which she'd paired with black linen pants and strappy taupe sandals. Appropriate for a casual evening and warm enough for the cool summer night. Around her neck she wore the ruby pendant her parents had given her for her eighteenth birthday.

"Hi, Lilly. Come have a seat!" Jack waved her over to the patio.

She smiled and said hello to everyone as she sat in a vacant chair. Paul turned, caught her eye, and broke into a wide grin.

"Hey, there! I was beginning to think you weren't coming. What are you drinking?"

"Just some Chardonnay, thanks."

"Coming right up."

Was it her imagination, or had he winked at her?

"It's nice to see you again, Lilly." He handed her a glass and sat in the empty chair next to her. Their eyes locked briefly. She wondered if he could tell how much she longed to talk to him . . . privately.

Charlotte, who had gone into the kitchen, reappeared with a tray of appetizers. "It's just going to be the six of us," she said as she passed them around. "Stewart and his wife had to cancel. Their youngest is running a fever."

They talked about parents, children, jobs, and summer vacations. Charlotte and Jack were sailing to Martha's Vineyard the next day and invited both couples to join them. They moved to the picnic table when the food was ready, and the years magically slipped away. They were all best friends again. Jack, who hadn't grown up summering in Mattapoisett, fit right in.

Lilly sat next to Paul during dinner and felt a physical spark when his arm brushed against hers while he passed the serving platter. Charlotte had suggested they dine outside at the picnic table. It was nice sitting outside, if a bit cramped. Lilly was sandwiched between Paul and Charlotte, while Jack, Sarah, and James sat opposite them. It was impossible to avoid physical contact as they enjoyed their meal, with Lilly's leg and shoulder constantly grazing against Paul's.

Occasionally they would catch each other's eye while the others were speaking. Paul reminded them about Lilly's eighteenth birthday and the fun they had that day at the regatta and the clambake before he left for Vietnam a few days later.

They all laughed as James recalled how Lilly fell into the water which cost Roger and Paul the trophy. As soon as James mentioned Roger's name, he stopped abruptly and looked at Lilly and Paul, his face flushed.

"I'm sorry. I shouldn't have brought that up."

"No worries, James," she assured him. "Those were good days—for all of us." She looked at Paul for confirmation, and he gave it with a nod and a smile that looked a bit forced.

After dinner they moved back to the patio fire to have dessert, which included a chocolate cake Lilly had brought from the market as well as the Italian wedding cookies Sarah brought. Jack had made a tape of music that had been popular during the summer of 1969 . . . "Good Morning Starshine" . . . "Wedding Bell Blues" . . . "Crystal Blue Persuasion" . . . in honor of the last time they'd all been together. Lilly felt her cheeks growing warm when the British group Mercy sang one of Lilly's favorites from that era, "Love Can Make You Happy." *How true those words were*, she thought.

Lilly sensed the evening was coming to an end, and she wondered if she'd get the chance to talk to Paul alone when it was time to leave.

Sarah and James were the first to leave; they didn't want to keep their babysitter up too late. Lilly took that as her own cue to say goodnight. After hugging them goodbye, she turned to Charlotte and Jack and thanked them for the wonderful evening. Paul stood at her side, her sweater in his hand. She had taken it off when the fire made her warm.

He gently placed the sweater around her shoulders as if he had done so a hundred times before, then said the words she'd been hoping to hear all evening.

"I'll walk you home, Lilly."

She was relieved that they would now have time to talk alone.

"Thank you."

The two of them started down the familiar dirt road lined with roses. He took her hand. They walked in continued silence for a few minutes before he cleared his throat and began to speak.

"I'm sorry you left last night before we had a chance to talk, Lilly."

"You seemed more interested in talking to everyone else but me."

He stopped walking and they stood under one of the few streetlamps on the road. She looked up at him, wondering what he was about to say.

He pulled something out of his pocket. It was a piece of paper—no, an envelope.

"I guess I was still trying to process seeing you again, which is why I kept my distance last night. I've been waiting to talk to you for twenty years. I was hoping one day I would have the chance to give this to you."

She stared at the envelope. "What is it, Paul?"

"This is the letter I wrote to you the day I landed back on American soil in 1973. I always thought you would wait for me, Lilly. That was what kept me going while I was in captivity. I made a promise to you that I would do everything I could to come back to you. The promise I made to you became my purpose every day for five years."

Lilly looked up at him and her lips began to quiver. The thought of him being held prisoner all those years brought back an incredible wave of pain and sadness.

"It must have been awful for you."

"It was. But no matter how hard some days were, I kept telling myself I needed to be strong for you, and for my parents, and for our future. I kept my promise to you, Lilly. I never understood why you didn't wait for me. I know it must have been very hard on you, but I thought what we had was special. I never thought I could be replaced so easily and so quickly. And by Roger, of all people."

She wanted to tell him the truth about Kate, and the pressure she felt from her parents and from Roger to get married. But she had to be certain he would understand. She knew once she said the words there could be no taking them back.

"I'm so sorry, Paul. I wish I could change the past. I wish I hadn't given up hope that you were alive." Tears rolled down her cheeks. "I was devastated when you went missing. Roger was, too. Our shared grief brought us together."

Was she imagining it, or had his eyes begun to water? She

had never seen Paul cry—he was always so confident, brave, and strong.

"He comforted me . . . but I never stopped loving you." She hung her head. "Roger eventually realized that. We stayed together for a long time, but without real love for each other, our marriage was troubled from the start." She raised her head, her eyes silently begging him to understand.

He held out the envelope. "I want you to have this letter. I want you to know that my feelings for you never changed. It's important to me that you know how much you meant to me. You kept me alive all those years. I don't know if seeing you these past two days has been good or bad for me. It brought back a lot of wonderful memories. But it also hurts. The pain of losing you is still there. I mailed this letter to you as I was boarding the bus to come home from Fort Bragg. I tried calling your house in Brookline, but your parents weren't home. I wanted you to get this letter before I got home so you would know I was coming for you."

"I never knew you wrote to me, Paul. I never even knew you were home or that you were alive until yesterday, when Charlotte called me. No one mentioned you to me, probably because they knew it would be an uncomfortable subject." She sighed. "I would have changed my life for you had I known. I don't understand why I never received your letter."

"It was returned to me at my parents' house along with a note from your mother."

She gasped in disbelief.

Paul stood under the lone streetlamp, and she read her

mother's note. Lilly leaned in as he read, recognizing her mother's beautiful cursive handwriting and powder blue stationery.

Dearest Paul,

We are so happy and thankful that after all these years you have come home safe. I wept with joy when your mother called us to share the news. We have been praying for you.

However, I am returning the letter you wrote to Lilly unopened.

Lilly is married to Roger Wentworth now and living with him and their daughter in Mount Kisco, New York.

I thought you should know. Stay well.

Fondly,
Florence Conroy

"She never told me about the letter, Paul." Lilly's voice relayed how frantic she felt—and the urgent need to tell him everything . . . right now.

"I believe you, Lilly. Your mother made it pretty obvious she didn't want you to know I had come home—but left it up to me to decide what to do."

Lilly nodded.

Guilt overwhelmed her as she thought of Paul being held as a prisoner of war for five years and then finding out she wouldn't be there to meet him when he returned. She would never forgive herself for not waiting for him.

He folded the letter carefully and put the envelope back in his pocket. She couldn't believe he had held onto that letter for all these years.

"The note from your mother was her gracious way of letting me know that things had changed, that life had gone on while I was away. You'd gotten married, had a child. I'm sure she knew why I was writing to you. She knew I wanted to see you. She left the decision up to me. I respect her for that. But as soon as my parents told me you had married Roger . . . my heart went cold. I just couldn't believe it, Lilly."

Lilly couldn't respond. She didn't know what to say.

"Anyway, I held onto that letter all this time. I guess it's because I wrote it on such an important day. I was free. I was coming home. I was going to see my parents again. I was going to see you and begin our life together. I was excited and happy to be coming home to you. I was finally going to marry you. And then, before it began, I received that note from your mother and realized the life I had planned for us together was suddenly over."

"Oh, Paul! You have no idea how sorry I am that our lives turned out this way. I want you to know I honestly never knew you were home. I would have left Roger in a heartbeat and come back to you." She reached for his hand and gave it an urgent squeeze.

"Let's walk down to the beach to sit and talk. There's so much I want to tell you."

They cut across the road and walked over to the beach and along the shoreline until they were well away from the cottages that sat along the shore.

She bent to take off her sandals. He kicked off his loafers and they started down the beach.

The moon shone full and high above the ocean, casting a shimmering light across the water and the beach. Their hands brushed against each other a few times before he captured hers. For a few minutes they walked in silence, then he stopped and turned to her.

"Let's sit here, Lilly." He placed his jacket on the sand for her to sit on, then sat beside her. He looked into her eyes, and she knew he was waiting for her to speak.

In a quivering voice, she began to talk.

"Paul, you need to understand how I felt. When I learned you'd been declared missing in action and were presumed dead, I didn't want to go on living. It was as if I had died, too, and nothing mattered anymore. I had nightmares that lasted for months. I woke up crying for you. I couldn't stop thinking about you, wondering if you were dead or alive. My heart broke for you—and for us."

Paul shook his head ever so slightly. "I'm still trying to understand, Lilly. I know you struggled, and I worried about you too. But I kept thinking back on our promise to each other. I promised you that I would come back. I did everything I could do to stay strong; no matter what happened I wouldn't give in. If I gave up—it would mean losing all that I had to live for. I just never thought you wouldn't be there for me when I got back. I just don't understand how you could marry Roger. I just don't get it. I've never been able to get that idea out of my mind, no matter how hard I've tried to understand. The only thing I could think of was that your feelings for me weren't what I thought they were. How could you have loved me the way I loved you if you would end up with him—of all people?"

Lilly had wanted to tell him everything—that she was utterly lost without him and needed a path forward for her and the baby—but instinctively she held back. She couldn't tell him about Kate . . . at least not yet.

"Did you love him the way you loved me?" Paul demanded. "The thought of you kept me alive for years, Lilly. The hope that one day we would be together again . . . married, raising a family and then to learn that you'd married my best friend and given *him* children . . . it just about killed me." His voice cracked with emotion.

Lilly sought to comfort him and touched his arm.

"No, Paul, I never really loved Roger. Don't you understand? When I lost you, I knew I would never love another man that way . . . so what difference did it make *who* I married? I wish you could know how I felt all those years ago. One minute you were asking me to marry you, and within a few short months I thought you were dead. That it was over. That you were never coming back. I cried every day for months. I dropped out of school. Lost focus. Lost my desire for living. There were weeks when I didn't even care if I got out of bed. Nothing mattered to me anymore, Paul.

"My parents wanted me to move on with my life. Roger was grieving for you, too. He started coming to visit me and became a shoulder to cry on.

"I was lost, and he promised he would take care of me. It didn't really matter to me one way or the other; I felt dead inside.

"My parents kept encouraging me to move on. They thought marrying Roger would help me get over you. I never did.

"The best I could do was be a good wife to him, set up dinner parties for his business associates and prospective clients, be a good mother. Eventually, he knew what we had was essentially a marriage of convenience. I did what I could to be good to him, but love was never part of the package. When Roger finally realized that, our marriage started to fall apart."

She lowered her head at the sadness of it all. *Three lives, wasted.* She wanted to bury her face in her hands and weep but she told herself she wouldn't. Instead, she lifted her head, swallowed, and said, "No one told me you were alive, Paul. Not my parents, and not Roger. I haven't been in touch with Charlotte or any of our old friends from Mattapoisett since the summer you left, and no one reached out to me once I left. I never wanted to come back here after you were gone—it was too painful for me."

He nodded. "This is a lot to come to terms with, Lilly, but I do believe you. I think I finally understand now."

Lilly was relieved to hear him say that. She thought of Kate. She was her reason for living in those early years.

"The memories of you were killing me. The only thing that

mattered in my life after I lost you was Kate. She was the only reason I had for living."

"I always knew Roger wanted you for himself." Paul sighed. "You know, I went to your house in New York one day."

"You came to New York?"

"After I got your mother's note, I decided I still needed to see you. I decided to drive down to Mount Kisco. I was angry at you and Roger, but it wasn't about confronting you. I just needed to see you again. I'd thought about you for so long. I figured if I saw you and you looked happy—I'd be able to forget about you – and move on for good."

Lilly couldn't believe he had come to see her all those years ago in New York and she never knew.

"You came to the house? In Mount Kisco?"

"Yes. I got your address from the phone book. I parked across from the house next door and sat outside in my car for over an hour, just watching your house . . . thinking back on it now, I know it sounds crazy. And then you walked out the front door holding hands with your daughter. You were smiling and she was laughing. Roger followed behind you, and you kissed him before he got into the car and you gave your daughter a big hug. She got in beside him and they drove off. You waved to them, and then you turned to go back inside. That's when I saw that beautiful smile on your face again."

Lilly caught her breath.

"Seeing you happy like that, more than anything, made me realize that I didn't belong in your life anymore and I needed to move on. So, I headed back to Boston to catch my plane home. I decided to focus on my work—and get as far away as possible. The heartache never left, but over time it became easier not to think about what might have been." His eyes met hers. "Obviously, your parents thought it was best for you not to know I was home. But I can't help thinking about what might have been . . ."

Lilly nodded. As Paul said, her parents were only trying to protect her happiness.

"You don't know how many times I wished you had come home to me. I kept all your letters, including the last letter you sent me twenty years ago. I've read and re-read that letter a million times. I'm sorry I didn't have the faith your mother had. I tried to believe you were coming back but I just couldn't imagine it.

"Your mother was sure you were alive. *I* was sure you were dead. I know it's too late to do anything about it now; what's done is done. I just hope you can forgive me for marrying Roger. Please, Paul . . . will you forgive me?"

She forced herself to meet his eyes, but he couldn't possibly know that she was also pleading with him to forgive her for something else he didn't know.

He drew her into his arms and held her close.

"I forgive you, Lilly, and I'm sorry for all the sadness. I know it must have been very hard for you." He wistfully added, "I just wish I could go back in time and that things had turned out differently."

He kissed her neck, and she closed her eyes. His lips felt

warm against her skin. She held her breath in anticipation. Her body was trembling with excitement as they kissed and felt each other again. Only Paul could make her feel this way.

He pressed against her and she could feel his heart beating firmly against his chest.

She felt herself slowly descending downward as he lowered her to the sand. He held her tightly and stroked her hair as she lay back against the dunes. They were both filled with an intense desire that had never gone away. All the years of longing turned to lust as their kisses grew more passionate.

"I love you, Lilly," he cried out in a hoarse whisper. "I never stopped loving you."

She squeezed him and held him close after they made love to each other, and together they fell asleep wrapped in each other's arms.

Chapter 14

Sailing Along

P AUL HAD WALKED her home in the early morning hours. She quietly tiptoed upstairs to her room, reflecting on how some things had remained the same while other things had changed. Twenty years ago, she didn't want to wake her parents after spending the night with Paul, now it was her children who she didn't want to wake.

She fell asleep with a smile on her face and awoke the next morning feeling renewed and more alive than she had felt in years. Time and distance couldn't keep them apart.

After all these years, Paul was back in her life again, and everything finally seemed right with the world. All her adult life there had always been something missing—the love she lost when Paul went missing. And now she had a chance to start over again—with him.

But the feeling didn't last for long. She held a huge secret. And she had to figure out what to do.

She slowly sat up in bed and looked out the window. The sun

glistened over the water, and a gentle breeze blew through the curtains.

What a beautiful day for a sail to Martha's Vineyard, she thought . . . but she continued to feel uneasy just the same.

Charlotte had told her to bring Kate and John along, and while Lilly didn't want to leave her kids alone all day, she was reluctant to introduce her kids to Paul. Thinking about the secret she was still keeping made her anxious. *Would she really be able to have fun and enjoy the day knowing she was lying to Paul—and to Kate—and had been lying for over twenty years?* She knew she would need to talk to him privately and that it would be a very difficult conversation.

As she got out of bed, she heard John yelling from downstairs.

"Mom, can you make pancakes? I'm really really hungry!"

She turned and looked at the alarm clock on her nightstand. It was already seven-thirty, and they were due down at the dock by ten for the trip to the Vineyard . . . a trip that Kate and John didn't even know about yet.

She reached for her white cotton summer robe hanging on the back of her bathroom door and quickly brushed her hair before stepping out into the hall.

She went to the landing. "I'll be right there, John. Let's make blueberry pancakes!" He looked adorable, standing there with his hair tousled, barefoot, wearing bright blue swim trunks along with a ratty old T-shirt. He was tan from spending so much time at the beach and his hair had lightened up a bit. He looked so casual and relaxed. Lilly suddenly began to see that this summer in Mattapoisett was helping John heal as much as it was helping her. He needed a break from the stress of the divorce and the tug-of-war with his father over custody.

"Sounds good!"

"Is your sister up yet? I have something to tell you both."

Kate emerged from her bedroom, down the hall from Lilly's. She wore white shorts, a pale pink polo shirt, and tennis shoes. Her long blond hair was tied back in a ponytail, and she looked very athletic, fit, and trim. She held a small, gift-wrapped package and an envelope in her hand, which she handed to Lilly after kissing her cheek.

"I know this is late, Mom. The timing was off yesterday so John and I decided to cook *you* breakfast this morning as a belated birthday gift."

Lilly's hand flew to her heart. "Oh, how sweet!" She shook a playful finger at John standing below. "And you tried to get me to make you pancakes!"

"Ha-ha!" he said, grinning. "We made muffins—your favorite, blueberry! Plus, scrambled eggs and bacon."

"Well, let's eat!" Lilly bounded down the stairs, followed by Kate. The scent of fresh-brewed coffee wafted through the air.

She sat at the table—which had already been set—and beamed.

"Thank you, kids! What a wonderful surprise, breakfast made for me by my two most favorite people. I love you both so much!"

Kate and John sat down to join her and shared the platter of eggs and bacon. Lilly reached for a warm muffin as Kate passed the basket.

She opened the envelope Kate had handed her—it contained

a beautiful card with a photo of a sunset. She recognized Kate's lovely handwriting. Inside she wrote, "*To the best mom in the world from the luckiest kids in the world—happy birthday!*"

She signed her name at the bottom, followed by John's best attempt at a cursive signature.

"I wonder what this could be?" Lilly asked playfully as she unwrapped the box. She peeled away the tissue paper, revealing a beautiful sterling silver frame and a photo of the three of them taken in New York's Central Park on Mother's Day . . . one of the first fun weekends the three of them had after the divorce became final. The photo captured a special moment in time, when all three of them looked happy despite the turmoil of the divorce and custody battle.

"This is a beautiful photo of us. Thank you so much! I'm going to keep it on my nightstand. It'll be the first thing I see in the morning and the last thing I see before going to sleep at night. We all look so happy! That was such a fun day."

"We thought you'd like it," John said happily.

Kate reached for Lilly's hand. "Thanks for all you do for us, Mom! We love you."

Lilly patted Kate's shoulder and gave John's hair a loving tousle.

"I'm planning on going over to the tennis courts and to see if I can find anyone who wants to play a practice round," Kate said.

"What was it you wanted to tell us, Mom?" John asked.

Lilly temporarily forgot about Charlotte's invitation to go sailing. Kate's plans to play tennis initially came as a relief . . . but she wanted Paul to meet his daughter for the first time, and for Kate to see her father—even if neither of them was aware of their connection.

"Yes, kids, I almost forgot. We've all been invited to go sailing to Martha's Vineyard with some of my old friends today."

"Who else is going? Will there be other kids there my age?" John asked eagerly.

"Yes. There will be plenty of kids about your age, John, and I'm sure they are all very nice." She turned to Kate. "I think you'll enjoy it too, even if there's no one in your age group. My friends were hoping to meet you. Would you mind checking out the tennis courts another day?" Lilly held her breath waiting for Kate's reply.

Kate didn't hesitate. "Sure! I love Martha's Vineyard! I went about five years ago with Melissa and her family, remember? When are we leaving? Do I have time to change and put on a swimsuit and my beach cover-up?" Kate asked.

Lilly was starting to get excited about the day ahead and was glad that Kate would be coming along on the trip to Martha's Vineyard.

"Yes, you have time to change. I'll get dressed right after I finish eating. We should plan to leave in about a half hour."

"That sounds like fun, Mom!" John said. "Do you think your friends will let me help sail the boat?"

"I don't know about that, but I'm sure they'll have *something* you can help with. Just, please, put on a clean shirt!"

John looked down at his old T-shirt and reluctantly got up from the table to change.

After breakfast. Lilly took a quick shower and got dressed while the kids cleaned up the kitchen. She decided to wear her black one-piece bathing suit, a white linen cover-up, her new leather flip-flops, and a wide-brimmed straw hat with a blue-and-white striped ribbon.

She looked at herself in the mirror and turned to check her figure. She suddenly realized how much she wanted to look her best—not so much for herself as for Paul. She felt a flutter in her stomach as she descended the stairs with her straw beach bag, feeling equally excited and nervous. The "what-if" scenarios began to dance in her head.

What if Paul somehow suspected Kate was his . . . saw himself in her eyes? What if someone else did? She decided to brush aside those worries—at least for now.

She took a few slow, deep breaths and began to feel calmer. Lilly reached for the cooler on the bench near the back door, which she quickly filled with ice, lemonade, cheese, and fruit.

Lilly looked up at the clock. It was getting late. She yelled from the kitchen and felt a bit irritated that Kate and John were taking so long to change.

"Are you two almost ready to go? We don't want to be late!"

Kate and John came into the kitchen. Each grabbed a beach towel and chair from the back porch, following Lilly out to the driveway.

The three of them jumped into the Volvo and headed to the pier downtown, where the larger sailing vessels and yachts were moored.

When they pulled up to the marina, Lilly saw kids milling

about on the deck of Charlotte and Jack's boat. The boat, called *Charlotte Rules,* was a beautiful, wooden, fifty-six-foot Hinckley ketch with four main sails.

"Wow, that boat is awesome!" John's excitement grew as he saw Charlotte and Jack's boat and realized what a special trip this was going to be.

Lilly pulled into the parking lot and slowly maneuvered her car into the last spot in between two large pick-up trucks. It was a picture-perfect day for sailing and the lot was full. There were people bustling on the pier and loading their belongings into the sailboats docked along the pier.

She turned off the engine, grabbed her beach bag from the backseat, locked the car and together with Kate, headed toward the dock, with John following behind closely. He had been put in charge of wheeling the red-and-white plastic cooler.

Charlotte was the first to welcome them as they walked up the plank and boarded the boat, her arms outstretched. "I'm so excited you all could come with us today. John, you're going to have to wear a life vest for safety."

"But I can swim!"

"John," Lilly chided, "put on the vest. I'm sure all the other kids are wearing them." She understood, even if John didn't, that Charlotte and Jack were being responsible.

"That's right, they are all wearing life vests. It's the rule on our boat whether visitors are onboard or not," Charlotte said, handing John a bulky, orange life vest. "The kids just went below to grab a snack if you want to head below and get something to eat."

John immediately scampered off to join them. He'd already met Charlotte's boys, although he hadn't yet met Sarah's kids.

Charlotte beamed at Kate. "And you must be Kate! I've heard so much about you. I'm Charlotte—one of your mother's oldest friends here in Mattapoisett. I dated your Uncle Mark for a short time when we were in college."

"Hello, Mrs. Farris," Kate politely greeted. "Thank you for inviting us."

"You're so welcome—and please call me Charlotte. I'm just sorry that there's no one your age with us today. Your mom was the first among our group to get married and have kids."

Lilly swallowed nervously.

"Oh, that's all right," Kate replied. "I love sailing. My father has a boat at our summerhouse in Newport and I really enjoy being out on the water. This will be my first sailing trip of the summer. I've been away studying abroad."

"Well, come on, then. Let me introduce you to the rest of the crowd. We've all known your mother since she was a young girl. We're all old friends—and getting older by the minute!" Charlotte waved them toward the bow. Lilly allowed her eyes to wander a bit while introducing Kate to Sarah and James. She saw Jack adjusting the sails but didn't see Paul. *Had something come up? Had he decided not to come after all?* Her heart sank at the possibility.

She then brought Kate over to Jack and introduced them. At his suggestion, they moved to the back of the boat where there was more comfortable seating.

"Is Paul coming with us?" she casually asked Charlotte as she sat on one of the cushioned benches.

"I sure am!"

Lilly turned and saw Paul with one knee up on the stern as he turned to pull in the mooring lines that securely held the boat against the dock.

Her heart skipped a beat as he looked over at her. His gaze intensified. He looked so handsome in a light blue polo shirt with white shorts and weathered boat shoes. She felt like she was falling in love for the first time all over again.

The toned muscles of his forearms were on display as he worked to secure the lines. Jack was in the cockpit and shouting commands to his "crew" of friends as they set sail, tacked against the wind, and headed to Vineyard Haven Harbor, which was about twelve nautical miles east of Buzzards Bay.

Once they were underway, Paul dropped the line and approached the bench where Lilly and Kate were seated. He lifted his aviator sunglasses off his face with his left hand and extended his right toward Kate.

"You must be Kate. I'm an old friend of your mother's, Paul Fletcher."

"*Dr.* Fletcher," Lilly prompted.

Kate extended her hand and gave Paul a warm smile. "Hello, Dr. Fletcher. It's nice to meet you."

Lilly watched nervously as they shook hands. Nothing seemed awkward, and Kate's sunglasses concealed her eyes, but it occurred to Lilly that things were beginning to feel uncomfortable . . .

*   *   *

The children all came back up to the upper deck from the cabin area below, clamoring for Jack to let them sit in the cockpit and help steer the boat. Paul showed them how to let out the sails, then Jack let them take turns steering before Charlotte invited the younger kids to have lunch. Paul soon rejoined Lilly and Kate at the back of the boat.

Lilly listened intently as Paul asked Kate about her studies. Paul seemed intrigued by Kate's interest in art and shared stories of Lilly when she was a young girl.

"I've known your mother since we were teenagers. She was always drawing or painting. Even on the beach she'd try to mold the sand into sculptures. It sounds like you've inherited her artistic talent." With that, Paul placed his hand over Lilly's, and they smiled at each other.

When Lilly looked back at Kate, she noticed her daughter's eyes lingering on their hands before looking up. Kate's sunglasses didn't conceal the question Lilly knew was in her eyes.

Paul must have noticed it, too, because he removed his hand.

Kate cocked her head to one side. "Is there something going on between you two that I don't know about?" She smiled while she asked the question, and her tone seemed playful.

After exchanging a quick glance with Paul, Lilly spoke up

first. "Well, Kate, Paul and I have known each other a long time but haven't seen each other in over twenty years . . . not until the other night at the fundraiser. We've been reconnecting over the past few days."

"That's right, Kate," Paul echoed. "Your mother and I go way back. I hope you're OK with me spending time with her this week. We have a lot to catch up on. It's been a long time since we've seen each other."

Lilly held her breath as she waited for Kate's response. Was it too soon for Paul to suggest they were in a relationship? They hadn't really discussed what was happening or what the future would look like after he left Mattapoisett and returned to work.

Kate beamed. "Dr. Fletcher, if my mom keeps smiling the way she's been smiling all day today, then I'm all for the two of you spending time together. She deserves to be happy. Especially during her birthday weekend!" She stood. "I'm going to grab an iced tea. Can I get anyone anything?"

Jack yelled over from the cockpit. "I'll take a lemonade," while Lilly and Paul declined. Paul squeezed Lilly's hand as he watched Kate walk away and head down to the cabin below.

Paul turned to Lilly with a sheepish expression. "I'm sorry for wearing my heart on my sleeve. I didn't mean to give anything away or make her feel uncomfortable."

"Kate's a smart girl. I think she may already be aware that there is something going on between us. I don't think she's bothered by it. In fact, she seems happy to see that I am enjoying my summer here—and my life again."

Lilly wondered what was going on behind those shades. *Would Kate sense that Lilly was starting to feel uncomfortable and figure it all out?*

"She seems so much like you, Lilly," Paul replied. "You've raised her well. She's beautiful and obviously very smart and talented. You're so lucky to have her—and John. I know my parents wished they had grandchildren. I regret not having kids of my own."

A wave of guilt swept over Lilly. *The Fletchers had a grandchild, yet they didn't know it. Had she been selfish all these years to keep the truth from them?* She started to think about all those years when Paul was missing and the heartache his parents dealt with every day. They had a granddaughter who could have brought so much joy back into their lives—and yet Lilly never told them.

"It's not as if it's too late for you to be a father, Paul. And yes, you're right. I *am* lucky to be a mother and I remind myself to feel grateful every day for my children—they are the two most important gifts I'll ever receive. If it hadn't been for Kate and John, I don't know what I would have done or how I would have been able to greet each morning with any kind of happiness these past few years."

Paul patted her shoulder. She suspected that if Jack wasn't seated two feet away from them, he would have hugged her. "Let's not think about the past, Lilly. The future is all that matters now."

* * *

They dropped anchor in Chappaquiddick, where they took a quick swim before going for a walk through Edgartown. Edgartown was part of Martha's Vineyard that was once a major whaling port, with historic houses that had been carefully preserved. There were several yachting events happening in the harbor and music from a local band filled the streets. They stopped at the penny candy store, loaded up on bags of sweet treats, and spent the afternoon swimming at the public beach overlooking Oak Bluffs.

The kids were finally resting on their towels after building sandcastles with Paul, Jack, and James while the women went for a walk and did some window-shopping on Main Street.

"Well, it looks like you've worn them out!" Charlotte exclaimed as they returned from their walk and rejoined the group on the beach. "I think it's time we thought about packing up."

Jack agreed. It was late in the afternoon, and he wanted to make sure they were heading back home before the wind picked up and it started to get dark.

Lilly turned to John and the other kids as she began to put the buckets and sand shovels into the beach bag. "Let's pack up—it's time to head home!"

They all returned to the boat and set sail for Buzzards Bay.

About twenty minutes into the trip John came running over to where Paul and Lilly were sitting with Kate. "Dr. Fletcher, Mr. Farris says it's time to tack and wants me to help you bring in the sails. Can you show me how to do it? He says the boat's keeling and we need to bring them in now."

"I'll help too," Lilly said. Paul got up and headed to the boom with John to bring in the sails. She watched as Paul showed him how to tighten the lines.

Paul seemed to be really enjoying spending time with the kids. *What a wonderful father he would have been,* Lilly thought. It occurred to her that the longer she held onto her secret, the more she risked losing him again.

She had to tell him the truth. She didn't know if it was a good idea for Kate to know the truth right away . . . but she knew she could trust Paul not to say anything to her until they had time to figure things out. She wondered what was keeping her from telling him the truth and knew pretty quickly—if she was being honest with herself—that she was afraid he would be angry and would somehow blame her for all the years that were lost . . . all the years he missed being a father while Kate was growing up. Would he be able to accept the truth while still loving Lilly as much as he had before?

Lilly would have left Roger in a heartbeat if she had known the truth all those years ago. She thought Paul was dead. In her mind he was never coming back.

The boat sailed smoothly into the harbor as they cruised along and then tied up at the dock in the early evening. After saying their goodbyes and thanking Charlotte and Jack, Lilly, Kate, and John headed toward their car. Paul walked alongside them, carrying the beach bag and helping John wheel the cooler over the cobblestones.

"Dr. Fletcher, my mom said you were a really good sailor. Could you go with me tomorrow and show me how to race around the buoys in Buzzards Bay? I didn't do too bad in the July Fourth Regatta, but I got a little confused with the course and want to do better on Labor Day."

Paul looked at John with a smile on his face. "Sure. If it's OK with your mom, we can go out tomorrow morning!" He looked over at Lilly seeking her approval.

Lilly suddenly realized that Paul had never said how long he was staying in town. Kate and John would be leaving the day after tomorrow to spend a few days with Roger in New York. She wanted to find some time for them to be alone, so she could talk to him and tell him about Kate. She knew she couldn't let too much time pass. It wouldn't be right, and it wasn't fair to him. She wanted him to know the truth.

"How long will you be in Mattapoisett, Dr. Fletcher?" Kate asked, as if reading Lilly's mind.

"I'm leaving the day after tomorrow." He caught the distressed look on Lilly's face. "I never told you when I was leaving, did I?"

"No, you didn't. That's . . . too bad. The kids are leaving then, too. They're going to New York to spend some time with Roger."

"Kate," Paul said, "could you take John back to the car and start unloading the beach bag? I need a few minutes alone with your mother."

"Of course," Kate replied.

John seemed oblivious to the conversation that was unfolding but he dutifully followed Kate back to the parking lot.

Lilly handed Kate the keys. Paul took Lilly's hand and led

her a few yards away. They stood under a large oak tree near the park that bordered the parking area.

"I'm sorry I didn't tell you I'd be leaving so soon. We haven't had enough time together and it never came up."

"I'm fine, Paul. It just caught me off guard."

"I hate that I'm leaving so soon. I'm scheduled to go back to Ethiopia, but I plan to come back to see you as soon as I can, hopefully before the end of the summer."

"I'll be going back to New York in September."

"I'll fly into JFK. Tell you what—let's have dinner tomorrow night before I leave. How does dinner at the Mattapoisett Inn sound?"

"Sounds lovely." They briefly held each other and then she took his arm.

"C'mon, let's get back."

They went back to the car. Kate had started the engine and turned on the air conditioning, so the windows were up. Lilly stood outside the driver's door and turned to Paul. "And thank you for offering to take John sailing tomorrow."

"He's a good kid and I had a lot of fun with him today." A faraway look appeared in Paul's eyes. "I wish the past twenty years hadn't been stolen from us, Lilly. Maybe if things had turned out differently, we'd be heading back home with OUR kids."

Lilly could only give a weak nod. "I know, Paul. I wish things had turned out differently. See you tomorrow."

She couldn't get into the car and drive away fast enough. She had almost blurted out the truth—and it wasn't the right time. Kate and John were just a few feet away. She needed to wait until they were alone. She realized time was running out—but she would tell him at dinner the following night. She promised herself that she wouldn't let the night end without him knowing.

Chapter 15

A Morning Visit

THE NEXT MORNING Lilly rose early. She hadn't slept well and felt melancholy. Paul would be leaving the next day. It felt like time was slipping away all over again. It had only been a few days since she and Paul had reunited, but she felt like a whole new life had begun to unfold—a life full of happiness she never imagined she would ever have—a life with Paul.

She hated that he was leaving so soon, yet she knew he wouldn't be able to stay. At least not right now. He had commitments overseas. She wondered if he meant it when he said he would be back in a few weeks. She tossed and turned all night, wondering if and when they would be able to build a life together . . . and then there was the issue of Kate.

She began to second guess herself. Telling him about Kate was not going to be easy. Maybe it was a mistake not to have told him the night of Charlotte's dinner party . . . she worried he would never forgive her if she waited much longer.

She simply couldn't risk losing him again! She *had* to tell him before he left. That meant it had to be tonight, at dinner.

Lilly felt uneasy as she ate breakfast with Kate and John that morning. Her children were happily recounting their sailing trip—the swimming hole at Chappaquiddick where they jumped off the bridge and the ice cream sundaes they all enjoyed at the arcade in Oak Bluffs before sailing back to Mattapoisett.

"Mom, I really like Dr. Fletcher. He's fun!" John said as he buttered his toast. "He told me you sailed with him and made him lose a trophy during the July Fourth Regatta when you fell overboard—you never told me that story!"

Lilly smiled at the memory. "I sure did land in the water—and it cost us the trophy that year. I was sailing with Uncle Mark, and Paul was sailing with your dad. They were good friends."

Kate put down her coffee with a quizzical look on her face. "So, you and Dr. Fletcher were sailing partners?" She looked across the table at Lilly intently.

Lilly decided that giving a little information about her history with Paul might make it easier for Kate and John to accept him as part of their family and part of the future she was hoping they would create together—as a family.

"Yes," she said in reply to Kate's question. "Paul and I have known each other for a very long time. We started dating when I was in high school."

"So, what happened?" Kate pressed. "You broke up when you went to college?" she asked.

"Well, he got drafted and left for Vietnam a few months before I left for college."

"Dr. Fletcher served in Vietnam?" Kate suddenly looked serious. "He's lucky he made it back alive. That was a senseless war. I feel bad for all the soldiers that were unfortunate enough to be drafted during the Vietnam era. How long was he there?" Kate leaned forward, obviously intrigued and wanting to know more about Paul's past.

"Well, we didn't really break up. Unfortunately, he was captured just a few weeks after arriving in Vietnam. He was a marine, serving as a medic, and was trying to evacuate wounded soldiers from a battlefield when his helicopter was shot down. He was missing for a very long time." Lilly didn't want to say anything more, but Kate persisted.

"So, he was a prisoner of war in Vietnam? How awful! How long was he held captive?"

"About four or five years. I didn't know it at the time. We all presumed he was dead. It was a horrible time for his parents, his friends . . . and me," Lilly added softly.

The look on Kate's face told Lilly that she had begun to realize that Paul was more than a long-lost friend . . .

"And he and Daddy were friends?" Kate mused.

Lilly nodded over a lump that had suddenly formed in her throat. Her daughter was no dummy. Lilly dreaded what she would ask next.

Fortunately, John spoke up first. "Is Vietnam the place where all the soldiers got killed in the jungle?" He was unaware of the significance of the story that was unfolding at the table.

"Vietnam was a mistake—we never should have gotten into that war." Kate looked over at him and spoke with conviction. She was a die-hard liberal and had very strong opinions about politics.

"Thousands of American soldiers lost their lives for nothing, and innocent people were killed, maimed, and tortured . . ."

John suddenly caught on to the seriousness of the situation. He put his half-eaten slice of toast on the plate in front of him and looked at Lilly, as if needing reassurance. "So, Dr. Fletcher fought in the war and escaped?"

"Actually, he was released when the war ended," Lilly replied.

"Hey, anybody home?"

Lilly breathed a sigh of relief. She heard Paul's voice at the back door, calling out as he knocked on the screen door before entering the house.

"Good morning!" Paul approached them and walked over to the kitchen table, holding up a white square box. "I brought us all a breakfast snack from Honey Dew Donuts."

Lilly pointed to the chair beside her. "Come join us, sit down Paul! And thanks for the donuts. Honey Dew Donuts are the best."

Paul sat down and opened the box, revealing a dozen freshly baked donuts.

"Mmm, these look delicious," Lilly exclaimed as she reached for a powdered lemon donut. "How about some coffee, Paul?"

"I'd love some. But don't get up; I'll help myself." He began opening the cabinets in search of a mug.

"Cups are in the cabinet to the right of the sink."

He poured himself a cup of coffee and returned to the kitchen table. "It's a beautiful day for a sail, John! I'm hoping we pick up a little more wind so we can pick up some speed and have some fun out there."

"Yeah—I hope it gets really windy so we can go fast—but just make sure we don't capsize like Mom did that year she lost the regatta!"

"Don't worry, John, we won't capsize. And your mother was a very good sailor; it was the reckless crew in another boat that crashed into your uncle that landed her in the water. I'm sure that won't happen to you!"

Lilly sat quietly enjoying the moment as he continued chatting with the children—a moment she never imagined would ever be happening.

The scene unfolding in the kitchen suddenly seemed surreal. She crossed her arms and gave herself a hug, pinching her arm just to be sure this wasn't a dream. After all these years. If he only knew he was having breakfast with his daughter for the very first time.

They chatted a while, long enough for everyone to enjoy a donut—or in John's case—two donuts, a jelly and a glazed.

"Guess we'd better get moving if we want to catch the best part of the day, John," Paul prompted.

With that, John hurried up to his room to get his baseball hat. Kate also rose and grabbed her racket. She was heading to the tennis courts, as she had planned to do the day before.

"Oh, Kate!" Paul said. "I almost forgot . . . I have something for you." He reached in his pocket and handed Kate a picture.

"This is your mother's senior class picture. I've had it for a very long time. I didn't know if you'd ever seen it. You're only a few years older than she was in this picture, and you look a lot like her."

Kate looked at the photo and studied it carefully. He'd had it laminated, and it had a square imprint on it, as if he'd carried it in his wallet for a very long time.

"Wow, Mom, you look so young—and beautiful!" Kate said as she looked down at the photo of her mother in a pretty, yellow summer dress.

Lilly's heart jumped when Kate turned the photo over. She still remembered the message she had written to Paul all those years ago: *To my one and only love. Forever, Lilly.*

Kate suddenly looked uncomfortable, as if she was somehow intruding, and quickly handed the photo back to Paul.

"Thanks for showing me the picture, Dr. Fletcher. Mom said you were a prisoner of war for more than two years—that must have been a horrible experience for you—and your family. I'm so glad you made it home . . ."

"Thank you, Kate. I appreciate your concern, but I've put that part of my life in the distant past. It's better that way."

John came running back into the kitchen, wearing his Yankees baseball cap. "I'm ready, Dr. Fletcher. Bye, Mom!"

Paul leaned sideways and gave Lilly a quick kiss as John ran outside.

"I'll drop him off around noon. I have a few errands to run before I leave tomorrow. I've made dinner reservations for seven. Is that OK?"

Lilly nodded. "That sounds great. I'm looking forward to having dinner at the Mattapoisett Inn. I haven't been there for dinner in years."

After Paul left, Kate spoke up.

"He's so nice, Mom. I wonder why he never got married?"

For a fleeting moment Lilly was tempted to tell Kate everything right there and then, but of course, she didn't. She would tell Paul first so they could tell Kate together . . . at the right time and in the right way.

"Yes, he's a very nice man and always has been." She sighed and decided to gently begin sharing more about her relationship with Paul so it wouldn't come as a shock to Kate later when she found out Paul was her real father.

"I know it may be difficult for you to imagine me being with someone other than your father, but Paul was very special to me, Kate. He was my high school sweetheart and someone I've never forgotten."

Kate opened her arms wide and embraced Lilly. "Mom, I want you to be happy. I know how bad things were between you and Dad before he moved out. I think it's sweet that you've reunited with someone from your past. I don't have a problem with it, and neither does John. Dad's the only one who will have a problem, and Dad's the one who will have to get over it." She kissed Lilly's cheek. "I'll see you later!"

Lilly felt relieved to have Kate's approval and could see how mature her daughter was becoming. Kate loved Roger, but she understood the reason her parents were now divorced. She never once tried to convince Lilly to reconcile with him.

As Kate reached the back door Lilly suddenly remembered she needed a babysitter for tonight. "Oh, Kate, before you go . . ."

Kate turned.

"Can you watch John tonight? I probably won't be home until late, and despite what he thinks, he's not old enough to be left alone at night."

"Sure, Mom. I'll be home tonight. Stay out as late as you want!" Kate waved and headed out the back door.

With the children gone for a few hours, Lilly had the morning to herself. She decided to go into town and buy a new dress. She really hadn't brought much with her, and she wanted something special.

Chapter 16

A Night to Remember

PAUL AND LILLY arrived at the inn just as the sun was setting over the harbor. The elegant dining room was softly lit with candles, casting a warm glow over the white tablecloths and the beautiful summer flower arrangements at each table.

The maître d' held out Lilly's chair for her. As soon as they were seated, Paul reached across the table to take Lilly's hand, gazing deeply into her eyes. "Lilly," he said, "there's something I need to tell you."

Lilly's heart began to race as she waited for him to continue. She felt a mix of excitement, nervousness, and anticipation.

"Even after all these years apart, the minute I saw you walk into the yacht club a few nights ago, I felt that an immediate attraction and emotional connection to you. I have never felt that way with anyone else."

Lilly felt tears welling in her eyes as Paul continued. He held her hand in his and spoke quietly, but intently.

"These last few days have convinced me that my feelings for you have never died. I love you, Lilly, and I don't want to spend another day without you. I need to take a few weeks to sort out some things overseas. I know you understand that I can't just walk away from my responsibilities with Doctors Without Borders, but my contract ends at the end of next month. I intend to help them find a replacement for me and then look for a role here in New York or the Boston area. I figure you intend to stay in Westchester?" As she nodded, he said, "I have some connections at Columbia-Presbyterian Hospital, and I don't think it will take me long to find a permanent position." He broke into a sheepish smile. "Listen to me, making plans for us without even asking you how you feel." He shook his head. "I just know in my heart that you and I were meant to be together. I've never stopped thinking about you since that day at the bus station in Hyannis when you waved goodbye. That image has been playing in my mind over and over and over again for twenty years. Even though you married Roger, I never stopped loving you. You don't know how many times over the years I've thought about you. Wished you married me, like we planned, and that our lives had turned out differently—living together as a family with *our* children . . ."

Lilly swallowed hard while he kept talking.

"It broke my heart when I found out that you and Roger got married. For years I carried that anger and resentment. Part of the reason I never got married was because I felt I could never let myself trust another woman . . . and partly because I never met anyone who I loved the way I loved you. But I know I can't blame you. You didn't know I would be coming back. No one knew if I was dead or alive. As I've gotten older, I realize that five years is a long time when you're in your early twenties. You deserved to have the family you always wanted, but I'll never forgive Roger. He took advantage of your grief. But that's all in the past now, Lilly. You're not married to him anymore. There's nothing I want more now than to start over with you, so we can share our lives . . . the way it was always meant to be." He smiled at her. "And now that I've poured my heart out . . ." his eyes asked an unspoken question.

Lilly felt a surge of emotion as she realized she couldn't tell him about Kate—not tonight. She couldn't risk losing him again . . . she wouldn't let the past ruin the present. But she was definite about her feelings. "Oh, Paul! I love you. I've never stopped loving you. And want to start thinking about our future plans together too. I don't want to spend another day without you—we have a lot of time to make up for."

They leaned forward and shared a tender kiss, then spent the rest of the evening lost in each other's company, making plans, enjoying the fresh seafood and admiring the beautiful views of Mattapoisett Harbor. After they finished their meal, Paul suggested they take a walk on the beach.

The sand was cool beneath their bare feet as they strolled along the shore, the moon reflecting off the gentle summer waves. They walked hand in hand, pausing every now and then to admire the full moon and kiss.

"I think we're getting a little too old to be making love on the beach. Let's go back to my hotel and enjoy a proper night together."

She laughed and playfully taunted him. "Well, you know I have children waiting for me at home. I will need to head back before the clock strikes twelve and I turn into a pumpkin."

"Don't worry, Cinderella, I already told your oldest not to wait up. I let her know I was planning a special evening for us and that we would be staying at the Mattapoisett Inn."

Lilly wrapped her arms around his waist and looked up at him. She was thrilled they would finally be able to spend the whole night together—it had been too long.

When they returned to town, they went directly to Paul's hotel room. The moment the door closed behind them; he pulled Lilly in close. They kissed passionately, their bodies pressed against each other as they gave in to their desires and made their way to the antique four-poster bed.

They tore at each other's clothes like young lovers, caressing each other, kissing each other, and pleasing each other in new ways. The heat was on as their passion for each other burned and they lay intertwined, giving into their desire for each other like never before, wrapped in the soft white summer satin sheets.

Afterward, as they lay in bed wrapped in each other's arms, they both knew they had found love again.

As Lilly drifted off to sleep that night nestled in Paul's warm embrace, she was totally satisfied and content. There was something undeniably special about the way he held her, a gentle strength that made her feel secure and cherished.

In his arms, she found not only comfort but finally felt like she was letting go of the past – and all the hurt and pain that Roger had caused her.

She felt at peace, knowing she had finally found what was lost all those years ago.

Her heart had found its home again.

She would tell him about Kate in the morning. The word *love* kept running through her head. Would he still *love* her after she told him about Kate? He had been so angry and resentful for so long after he found out she married Roger. She wasn't exactly sure what to expect but that didn't change the fact that he deserved to know the truth. It was time to tell him.

Chapter 17

Morning Rush

THE NEXT MORNING Paul and Lilly enjoyed an early morning breakfast together on the porch at the inn. They had to rise early because she had to take Kate and John to the train station. They were going to spend a few days with Roger in upstate New York.

Lilly and Paul watched as the sun rose higher over the harbor. Lilly was grateful for the night they had shared together, but sad that he would be leaving so soon. They had lost so much time . . . she worried that what they had found could be lost again.

"You seem quiet this morning," Paul noted as he helped himself to another piece of toast. "Are you OK? Or are you just tired from all the fun we had last night?"

She took a sip of coffee before replying. "I'm just thinking about the fact that everyone is leaving today. First the kids, and then you."

"But we'll all be back, Lilly. Didn't you say the kids would only be gone for a few days?"

"Most of the week, actually." She sighed. "I have a feeling they're going to tell Roger about meeting you."

"Are you saying you'd rather be involved with someone else?"

"No, never!" Lilly appreciated his effort to put her at ease. "I'm going to the ladies' room. But speaking of the kids, we should probably get going before they begin to wonder if I'm ever coming back. I'm going to take them to the train station in Providence. There'll be less traffic than going to Boston."

"Sure. I'll get the check and meet you outside. In the meantime, start thinking of where you want to spend our honeymoon."

That thought made Lilly smile. She reached for her sweater draped on the back of her chair and grabbed her purse. She leaned over spontaneously and softly kissed his cheek. "Thanks for a wonderful night, honey."

As she walked away, she felt him watching her.

Chapter 18

The Bitter End

THEY DROVE ALONG the shore road with the windows down and listened to the radio. They were playing an oldies station and laughing as they sang along with their old familiar favorites.

Their conversation flowed effortlessly, their laughter echoing in harmony.

She felt young again – the way she had felt all those years ago when they would drive around town in his car, their laughter echoing in harmony.

Paul turned and pulled into the driveway. Lilly gasped at the sight of the familiar black convertible BMW sedan parked beside the house.

It was Roger's car.

"What's the matter, Lilly?" Paul said, his voice ringing with concern. "You look like you've seen a ghost. Whose car is that?"

"It's Roger's." She quickly turned down the radio and reached for her purse.

"But didn't you say you were sending the kids to New York on the train? Why is he here?"

"I'm not sure, but I can only guess. John was so excited about going sailing with you . . ."

"You think he called Roger and told him about it . . . and about me being here?"

"Yes. Maybe you should just go back to your hotel and let me deal with him. I know he won't be happy to hear that I was out all night with you. I don't want to cause a scene."

"No, Lilly. The only place I'm going is in the house with you. I don't care if he's upset or angry. He needs to know we're a couple now, and I'm actually looking forward to telling him to his face that whatever you two had is really over."

Lilly felt a sense of dread overtaking her. She reluctantly got out of the car and took Paul's hand as they approached the front door of the cottage.

She dreaded the exchange she knew would follow but couldn't come up with a good reason to disagree with Paul.

Lilly stepped into the house and walked to the kitchen, where Roger sat at the table eating breakfast with Kate and John. The radio played softly in the background.

"Mom!" John cried out. "Daddy's here. He drove up and surprised us this morning. We don't have to take the train back to New York; we'll be driving!"

"Yes, I see."

Kate beamed at Paul. "Good morning, Dr. Fletcher."

"Good morning, Kate . . . John . . . Roger."

Roger slowly turned around in his chair. *He looked tired,*

Lilly thought. His face was puffy, and he had dark circles under his eyes. Lilly suspected he'd had a lot to drink last night. It was barely nine o'clock in the morning. He must have left New York before dawn.

"Welcome back, Paul," Roger replied, adding, "You're looking well. It's been a long time."

Lilly picked up on the sarcasm in his voice. She squeezed Paul's hand tightly as Roger spoke. She was grateful that Paul was by her side and began to realize that this confrontation was inevitable.

Roger stood and faced them. "I thought you were working overseas, Paul. It's nice to see you after all these years." He stretched out his arm in an offered handshake. Paul slowly obliged and moved forward to shake his hand.

"What brings you back to Mattapoisett?" Roger's eyes slid to Lilly. "Actually, I guess that's a dumb question."

"Kids," Lilly said quickly, "Why don't you get your bags and put them in the car? You don't want to keep your father waiting. Kate, please make sure John has packed his toothbrush and a few bathing suits."

"OK, Mom." Kate took John's hand and led him to the stairs. She turned and gave Lilly a worried look. Lilly forced a smile, nodded, and gestured for her daughter to go up and get the bags, then turned to face her ex-husband.

"Roger, the kids will be ready to go in just a few minutes. Why don't you just wait outside in the car?"

Roger didn't move. Instead, he looked at Paul directly. "I know you came back for Lilly. I'll bet you couldn't wait to get back here once you found out she was finally a free woman. Or maybe you two planned this little rendezvous a long time ago. Is that why you really wanted the divorce, Lilly? So, you could run back to Paul and live happily ever after?"

Paul calmly replied, "Let's be civil, Roger. I just came in to say hello to you. We can sit down and have a talk another time."

Roger took a step closer, a smirk on his face. "Another time? How about right now? John told me last night you'd taken him sailing, and when I got here Kate told me you two went out for dinner last night and spent the night at the Mattapoisett Inn. Do you think that's setting a good example for my kids? They're *my* kids, you know. I raised them. They'll always be mine. You can't take them away from me."

"I'm not trying to take them away from you, Roger. We're adults. Let's just wish each other well and talk about all this another time. I don't want to upset Lilly or the children. There's no need for you to make a scene."

Lilly watched helplessly as Roger turned his attention to her. She feared a jealous rage was beginning to boil. While he had never been a violent man, he was very bitter about the divorce, and learning she was with Paul was probably more than he could handle. She fought back the urge to grab Kate and John and drive away.

"Did you two have this little reunion planned all along?" Roger snarled. "Tell me the truth. Is that why you wanted to come back here, so you could be with him?"

Lilly stood her ground. "That's ridiculous, Roger. Paul didn't arrange to meet me here in Mattapoisett. He had no idea I'd be here, and more than that—I had no idea he was still alive. You're acting crazy, and you need to stop it."

"Did he forgive you for marrying me?"

"Roger, you're acting irrational. Please, just stop it," Lilly pleaded.

Paul moved in front of Lilly, a protective act she found comforting. He and Roger stared at each other like two boxers facing off in a ring. She hoped Roger would calm down. Paul was in great physical shape. Roger was in no condition to get into an altercation with him.

Lilly heard the kids coming down the stairs. She turned and gestured to them to bring their bags outside. Paul and Roger stood staring.

Roger's voice dripped with sarcasm. "So protective. But I'm sure if he knew the truth, he wouldn't be so happy to have you back, Lilly. Does he know you've been lying to everyone these past twenty years?" Roger's gaze moved from Lilly to Paul.

Paul turned to Lilly for a brief moment, a quizzical look on his face, before Roger drew his attention away from her.

Sweat coated Lilly's palms, and her heart pounded in her chest. *No, Roger, don't! Please don't . . .*

"She lied to me the whole time we were married," Roger continued. "She pretended to love me when she didn't. She lied to the world about Kate because she was too afraid to be alone when you went missing in action. You left her alone and pregnant."

Paul turned to Lilly in disbelief.

Roger continued. "Why don't you just admit it, Lilly? You

lied to me. You've lied to him, and you and I have both lied to Kate since the day she was born. Well, maybe it's about time we all told the truth."

Lilly grabbed Paul's hand and squeezed it, tears streaming down her face. "Paul, I—"

"Lilly, is this true? Is Kate *my* daughter?"

Roger went on. "I was a good friend to you, Paul. When you went MIA, I stood in for you. I'll tell you what I should have told you fifteen years ago when you came home." His words were coming out rushed, as if he couldn't wait to say them. "That's right, Lilly was pregnant when you left for Vietnam. Kate is your daughter. Didn't you notice her beautiful blue eyes? I've looked into those eyes every day for the last twenty years. I've loved Kate since the day she was born, but she was a constant reminder of you, and I'm sure Lilly felt the same way." His shoulders slumped momentarily in defeat. "I married Lilly because I loved her . . . but we could never escape your presence. You can take Lilly from me, but you'll never get back the years I've had with Kate. She's as much mine as John is."

Lilly studied Paul's reaction. His features hardened before her eyes as he absorbed Roger's words. His hand felt cold as he let go. She didn't know what to do or what to say. He knew everything now, and what started as a beautiful morning had suddenly turned into a very dark day.

Roger was practically taunting Paul. He started to move forward, as if to take a swing at him, but Paul quickly grabbed him by the collar.

"I don't want to hear any more from you, Roger. You may have stood in for me, but don't expect me to thank you for taking care of Lilly all these years. I don't believe you were a good husband to her, and I have to wonder just how good a father you were to Kate. I think you're selfish and self-centered. You were always competing with me when we were growing up. I knew you always wanted Lilly, because she was the one girl you could never ever have. She was mine. She was never really yours—and you know it."

"Paul, please let him go," Lilly pleaded. She'd never seen that fiery look in Paul's eyes before.

Paul released his hold on Roger's collar and yanked him backward. Roger managed to quickly regain his footing after a slight stumble.

"It's time for you to leave Roger." He rushed past Lilly and Paul with a scowl on his face as he left.

He turned to face them as he reached the door. "The kids will be back Thursday. And I won't say anything to Kate—at least not yet." Then he left.

"Wait!" Lilly clutched Paul's forearm as she ran to the back door. "I have to say goodbye to Kate and John."

She ran outside and waved as they backed out of the driveway.

"I love you both. I'll see you in a few days!"

They waved from the car and once they had turned down the road and were out of sight, she returned to Paul who was pacing in the kitchen, running his fingers through his hair, and shaking his head.

"Lilly, I'm going to check out of my hotel. I need time to think about all this," he said.

"When will you be back?" she managed to ask.

"I'm not sure. I need time to think. To be honest, I'm numb." He stared at her, shaking his head in disbelief. "Why didn't you tell me about Kate?"

"I was going to. I was just waiting for the right time. Actually, I was going to tell you this morning; I swear I was. It seemed like the right time, what with the kids leaving and . . . and you leaving, too." She paused, a question burning in her heart. She had to ask.

"What do you mean, you don't know when you're coming back? I thought we were going to make plans." Her eyes searched his face for understanding.

"Lilly, you broke my heart a long time ago, and I've been running away from you ever since. Now here I am standing next to you twenty years later and my heart is breaking all over again. We had a daughter I never knew about. It's hard for me to process this. The scars run deep. I need time. It's taken me a long time to understand why you married Roger . . . and now I find out Kate is *my* child." He slowly shook his head. "You say you were going to tell me, but I'm not sure that's really true.

Why didn't you tell me the first night we sat on the beach together and talked? I'm not sure I can ever believe in you again—or trust you. How could you let me spend time with her this week and not tell me that she was *my* daughter – that she was *ours*?"

Lilly felt her whole world crumbling. Paul's words crushed her. *If only I'd told him instead of putting it off . . .*

Paul slowly backed away, taking one long look at Lilly before turning toward the door. She waited until he left to run after him, reaching the backyard in time to see him in the driveway. His head turned to look at her from the car, and for one brief moment their eyes met and she felt a glimmer of hope . . . but then he turned away and drove off.

She fell to the ground and began sobbing. How could this be happening? She felt the same way she did twenty years ago—her life as she knew it was ending. For a few short days she'd been so happy, had even started to dream those same dreams . . . of a future with Paul.

She slowly got up and walked into the kitchen. As she walked down the hallway, the silence in the house was practically palpable. She headed upstairs and laid on her bed, thinking of the letter her mother had sent back to Paul all those years ago. If only her mother had told her that Paul was home and had come back for her . . . how differently her life would have turned out.

It seemed such a cruel irony that the daughter she and Paul had conceived together—the one piece of him she had held onto all this time—would be the reason they were torn apart again.

*   *   *

The rest of the summer slowly dragged on. Kate, like John, made new friends in town but for Lilly every day began with hopeful anticipation that she would hear from Paul, either by mail or by phone . . . and every night she went to bed anxious and disappointed. His image lingered in her mind.

Would he ever come back to her? Didn't he want to have a relationship with the daughter he never knew he had? How could he blame her for what happened? Didn't he realize that she was as much a victim of timing and circumstances as he was?

Lilly tossed and turned each night, more questions and "what-ifs" running through her head as each day passed. If only Roger and her parents had told her the truth and that he had come back to find her . . . it hurt to even think about what might have been. It wasn't fair for Paul to hold her responsible for a twist of fate neither one of them could have controlled. She knew in her heart that she wouldn't have held on to the secret forever. She was planning to tell him the truth that day. If only he believed her. Lies, lies, lies . . . those words kept running through her head. Did he think she would have continued lying to him about Kate? Her parents may have lied to protect her. Roger may have lied to protect himself, but Lilly had no reason to keep the truth from Paul. Didn't he realize that? If only he would call her or write to her so she could explain and reassure him again.

Chapter 19

Labor Day

AS THE SUMMER drew to a close, Kate, Lilly, and John began to pack up the cottage. Most of the families who lived in the Boston area would spend weekends in Mattapoisett through October, but it was too far to travel from New York. And besides school would be starting soon, Kate would be heading back to NYU, and Lilly intended to look for a job.

Lilly had been feeling listless lately but was slowly accepting the fact that maybe he was never coming back.

The only person she had confided in over the past month was Charlotte. She told her everything—about how she found out she was pregnant shortly after Paul was declared MIA and that she thought marrying Roger was the right thing to do. She admitted to Charlotte that she and Paul still loved each other and that they had started to make plans for their future until it all exploded when Roger showed up and told Paul about Kate before she had found the chance to talk to him about it.

Charlotte expressed admiration and respect for all Lilly had been through, and sympathy for her situation. She insisted she was sure Paul would come around and that he just needed time to adjust and reflect on all that he now knew.

On the morning of Labor Day, Lilly and Charlotte were walking down the sandy road to watch the Labor Day Regatta when Lilly suddenly stopped.

"What's wrong?" Charlotte asked, concern in her voice.

"I'm sorry, Charlotte, but I think I need to head back to the house. I'm not feeling very good. I haven't been sleeping much these past few weeks, and I think it's starting to catch up with me."

Charlotte took Lilly's hand. "C'mon, I'll walk back to the house with you."

They turned around. Speaking hesitantly, Charlotte said, "Lilly, maybe you should go see someone ... you know, a therapist. You've been through a lot this summer. You said yourself you haven't been sleeping well, and you're tired all the time. I think maybe you're getting depressed."

"I don't think I need a therapist." Lilly managed to reply. "I think the sun and not eating enough these past few days is making me lightheaded and a bit dizzy."

"You didn't eat?"

"I just had a cup of coffee and a little juice."

Charlotte squeezed her hand. "When we get back to the cottage, I want you to sit on the porch and rest, and I'll make you a *real* breakfast."

Lilly was grateful for Charlotte's friendship. When they

reached the cottage, she did as her friend asked and sat in one of the Adirondack chairs facing the water. She could see the start of the regatta in the distance, the white sails dotting the horizon.

Charlotte went into the house and returned with scrambled eggs, fruit, and juice on an old wooden tray that Lilly's mother had often used to serve her father lunch on the porch.

She and Charlotte ate breakfast and sat on the porch as the race began and the boats came into view.

"I hope John does well today," Lilly said. "He's been practicing hard all summer." She tried not to think about how Paul had helped him the day before everything fell apart. She ate the last of her eggs and patted her mouth with a napkin. "That was delicious, Charlotte. I haven't had much of an appetite lately but this morning I was hungry and not feeling nauseous."

Charlotte looked at her sharply.

"What?" Lilly wondered what was on Charlotte's mind and questioned the look on her face.

"Lilly . . . I know you've been tired lately and feeling dizzy and lightheaded. Now, you say you've been nauseous. Do you think . . . do you think . . . is there any possibility that you could be pregnant?"

Lilly's mouth dropped open, and a hand rose to cup her jaw.

"Oh my God," she whispered. "I don't know why that hadn't occurred to me! I've always had irregular cycles, and with all the stress from Paul leaving . . ." She looked down at her flat stomach. "After the Regatta I'll go into town and buy a test. Oh my God, Charlotte. This is surreal. Twenty years ago I was pregnant, and Paul was on the other side of the world. How could this be happening all over again?"

"If you are, you'll have to tell him right away," Charlotte advised. "He might have a hard time understanding why you didn't tell him about Kate sooner—but he'll never forgive you if you don't tell him he has a chance to be a father again!"

"I don't even know how to reach him."

"Doctors Without Borders will know."

Lilly nodded. She couldn't help thinking, *if I am pregnant, maybe this baby is just what we need to bring us together.*

It was almost noon when Lilly got back from the drugstore with the test. Kate and John were out with friends and celebrating John's third-place finish in the regatta. She sat on the edge of the bed, staring at the plastic pregnancy test in her hand, waiting for the results. She watched as it began to show, and there it was, staring back at her with two pink lines.

She felt a mix of emotions—excitement, joy, fear. She loved being a mother, but never imagined she would have another child.

Charlotte was right—Paul had to know right away.

*   *   *

They drove back home to Mount Kisco the following day. Lilly threw herself into getting John ready for school. Kate's semester at NYU didn't start for a few days, but she had already started to pack and to make a list of the things she would need for her new off-campus apartment.

In the evenings, alone in her room, Lilly went over what she planned to say in her letter to Paul. She had asked Charlie Peck, who had organized the fundraiser for Doctors Without Borders, for Paul's mailing address and phone number, but decided a letter would give him more time to process the situation in his own way.

She had to believe he would respond to her. Maybe he could walk out on her for not telling him about Kate, but she found it hard to believe he wouldn't take responsibility for this baby. She realized it was harder given Kate's age to suddenly appear and be part of her life. Kate was older, which made it more complicated. But Lilly couldn't imagine Paul wouldn't want to show up and be a father to this baby once he found out she was pregnant.

*   *   *

Lilly sat at the old wooden desk in her bedroom, staring at the blank piece of paper. She had been thinking about just what to say to Paul, but nothing sounded right to her.

Finally, she took a deep breath and picked up her pen. *Just say what's in your heart,* she thought. Then she began to write.

Dear Paul,

It's been almost two months since we last spoke, but I wanted to write and share some news that you need to know.

I'll get right to the point.

I'm pregnant.

I guess those hot summer nights have brought us to a place neither one of us imagined we would ever be—but I hope with all my heart that this time we can welcome our baby into the world together.

I know a lot has happened between us. Life has been unfair—but I also know that neither one of us ever intentionally meant to hurt the other. I know there have been lies that kept us apart in the past, but I was always planning to tell you the truth about Kate.

I had planned to tell you at dinner at the inn, but when you told me how you felt and we started to make plans, I was so happy; I couldn't bring myself to tell you just yet. I promise you I was going to tell you after the kids left for New York. I would never have kept the truth from you—that Kate was your daughter.

Please give us one more chance to have the life we were meant to have together.

I know you may be angry right now and feeling bitter, but I hope our story isn't ending. I found true love a long time ago—with you.

Please come back to me . . . to us.

Love,
Lilly

She added her phone number, then read the letter over and over again.

After a few minutes of hesitation, she read the letter one last time before sealing the envelope and putting it in her purse. She would bring it to the Federal Express office in the morning. It would reach him in just a few days, and they would be able to track it and notify her when he had received it.

The next morning, she felt a sense of relief once the letter had been mailed. Now she would just have to wait. At least she had plenty to do to keep busy. It was almost time for Lilly to take Kate back to college.

Three days later she was in the garage getting boxes for Kate when the phone rang. It was early in the morning just after 7:00 a.m.—it would be 2:00 p.m. in Ethiopia—she had done the calculations. Maybe it was Paul! She ran to the kitchen to pick up the phone and was breathless when she answered.

"Hello?"

"Good morning, Lilly!"

It was Charlotte.

"I'm sorry to call so early but I haven't had a chance to check in and see how you're doing. It's been so busy getting all four kids ready for school this year. It seems the older they are, the more there is to prepare, but as I was pouring my morning coffee, I was thinking of you and couldn't wait another day to call. How are you? Did you hear from Paul? What did he say?"

Lilly was happy to hear from Charlotte but disappointed it hadn't been him. For one minute she was so sure it would be his voice on the other end of the phone . . .

But she needed to talk to someone. She had been driving

herself crazy all week, tossing and turning in bed every night and wondering why he hadn't called or written to her.

"I wrote him a letter four days ago but haven't heard from him at all."

"Well, four days isn't a long time. I'm sure it takes at least a week for mail to arrive in Ethiopia. After all, it's halfway across the world.

"I sent the letter Federal Express, Charlotte. I'm beginning to think it was all too much for him to absorb. He had been away a long time. Sure, maybe seeing each other brought back all those memories, but I don't know if he ever really got over the fact that I married Roger.

"And he left here feeling like he couldn't trust me—no matter how many times I said it I'm not sure he believed that I was going to tell him the truth about Kate. The way he looked at me when Roger told him Kate was his daughter and that I had been lying to him. He looked at me with such disappointment, bewilderment, sadness, and disbelief.

"I wish I could erase that scene in the kitchen from my memory. It's not how I wanted to say goodbye to him." Lilly could hear one of the kids in the background calling to Charlotte.

"I'm so sorry, Lilly. I hate hearing you like this; you sound so sad, but I am absolutely sure he will call the minute he receives your letter! There's no way he would just walk away from you, not now, not after everything you've both been through. I saw the way he looked at you. There's no doubt he is still just as much in love with you as he was twenty years ago."

"Well, that was a very long time ago, Charlotte. Maybe once he got back to work, he realized he couldn't just step back in time and start where we left off. That would be a lot to expect. It would mean turning his whole life around for me and for Kate and John. I'm sure he's still thinking about all the years he missed with his daughter. Those are years he'll never get back.

"It's been almost two months since he found out about Kate, Charlotte. They have phones in Ethiopia. I know he received my letter. I received a notification from Federal Express yesterday. I really thought he would call by now. I actually thought maybe it was him calling when I heard the phone ringing this morning. But now I'm not so sure. He ran away from this life a long time ago, maybe he's decided it's best for him to stay away."

"Well, just because he received the letter yesterday doesn't mean he's read it yet. Just be a little more patient, Lilly," Charlotte was doing her best to be upbeat. She seemed convinced that Paul would come back.

"Well, last night I couldn't sleep at all. I thought he would call yesterday. Maybe he doesn't want to start all over again. It still breaks my heart to think he wouldn't want to get to know Kate—and I don't think he trusts me anymore. He believed I would wait for him all those years ago. He was sure of it, and I disappointed him. I wasn't there for him, Charlotte. I broke my promise. He left here believing I wasn't being truthful—that I would have kept the truth from him about Kate.

"I was hoping he would be able to understand, that he would come back after finding out we have another chance to have a child, a baby that we would be able to love together. I just don't know what he's been thinking—but maybe this was all too much for him, Charlotte, I just don't know what to do anymore."

"I'm so sorry Lilly. I'll call you back in a few days to check in. Please get some rest. You have another baby on the way and need to take care of yourself."

Chapter 20

The Homecoming

L
ILLY WOKE UP early the next day to begin packing the cars for the drive to NYU. It was a warm day and still felt like summer. She decided to wear her favorite sleeveless sundress—a cream-colored cotton dress she had bought earlier in the summer. She looked in the mirror and realized how tired she looked. She hadn't slept in days.

She headed downstairs and out to the driveway where Kate was busily rearranging the boxes, clothes, lamps, and quilts that she was bringing back to school.

Kate's car was full, and so was Lilly's Volvo. Lilly wasn't feeling that well, hadn't slept, and was becoming impatient with John, who was riding his bike in circles on the driveway. He was restless and bored.

He had asked Lilly at least ten times if he could stay home.

"Why do I have to go with you? I want to stay here and ride bikes with my friends. It's the weekend, Mom!"

"John, we're going to stay overnight in the city, and you're too young to stay home alone. Besides, you can help us carry Kate's things to her apartment. We have a lot to do and we need your help."

"Well, I'm going to ride around the neighborhood until it's time to go."

"We're leaving in ten minutes so please make it a quick ride!"

John started to ride down the sidewalk while Lilly and Kate moved the rest of the boxes outside.

She and Kate were wrestling with the last remaining items. It was becoming increasingly obvious to Lilly that Kate needed to rethink what she was bringing with her.

"Kate, I think you've packed too much. You won't be able to see out the rearview mirror. Isn't there anything here you can leave behind? You can always pick up your winter clothes at Thanksgiving. You don't need to bring everything today."

"Maybe you're right, Mom. Let me see what I can pull out and leave behind."

Kate started to unload a few boxes and repack her suitcase on the driveway.

The sun was bright, and Lilly held one hand above her eyes to protect herself from the glare as she looked down the street hoping John was on his way back. They didn't have time to go looking for him—it was starting to get late.

She turned her head at the sound of an approaching car. A yellow taxi pulled up along the sidewalk in front of the house. She wondered who it was and if they were lost.

She wasn't expecting any visitors . . . and then the door opened. A man stepped out onto the sidewalk carrying a duffel bag. He was tall, with aviator sunglasses, and wore a pair of faded jeans and a black T-shirt.

It was Paul.

She wanted to run into his arms, hug, and kiss him and never let him go, but instead she froze.

She couldn't do that . . . not without knowing why he was here.

Maybe he just wanted to say goodbye face-to-face.

John rode up to him on his bike. "Dr. Fletcher!" He let his bike fall to the ground and ran to over to Paul, who was on the sidewalk paying the taxi driver.

Paul hugged him and looked over at Lilly as the taxi drove off.

"Mom, is that Dr. Fletcher? What's he doing here?" Kate paused from her packing and watched as Paul began to walk toward them with John following close behind on his bike.

Lilly stood motionless.

Paul met her gaze. As he got closer, she could see a smile on his face.

"Do you two need a hand with that?" He dropped his duffle bag and bent down to pick up one of the boxes Kate had repacked. He neatly placed it in the back of the car.

Lilly sighed with relief when he turned and held out his arms to hug her.

She felt his lips brush against her hair and heard him whisper quietly in her ear.

"Lilly, I'm so sorry I left you. I promise I'll never leave you again. This time I'm here to stay—if you'll have me."

She laid her head on his shoulder, looked up at him and gently replied in a soft voice, "I think you're stuck with me now. After all, you wouldn't leave a girl alone and pregnant—now, would you?"

"Never again!"

John dropped his bike on the driveway and came over to where Lilly and Paul were standing.

"Are you coming with us, Dr. Fletcher? We're taking two cars back to NYU because Kate has too much stuff!"

"Yes, John, I'll be coming along for the ride today. I think it's time we all got to know each other better.

"But before that, I have something very important to ask your mother."

Paul turned to her and took both her hands in his. He took a deep breath. "I love you, Lilly. You're the only woman for me. Will you marry me?"

She smiled at him, barely aware that Kate and John were standing close by on the lawn, watching what was unfolding in the driveway and eagerly waiting to hear what their mother would say.

"Yes, Paul. Nothing would make me happier than to spend the rest of my life with you." Her heart swelled with joy as she looked into his beautiful blue eyes and they kissed.

Kate and John came running over to join what was quickly became a group hug. Lilly felt a new bond forming that she knew would grow stronger with each passing day . . .

She and Paul had finally found their way back to each other.

Their happily ever after was late in coming, but this time she had no doubt it was here to stay. Their love story would continue to stand the test of time.

*   *   *

The End

Printed in the USA
CPSIA information can be obtained
at www.ICGtesting.com
LVHW061752160823
755283LV00008B/288/J